MIRACLE MAN

When the President elect of the Bureau of Advanced Science, Dr. Mark Haslam, encounters Esau Jones, he's astonished to learn that Jones can perform apparent miracles. Yet, despite his amazing gifts, Jones is content to remain anonymous, living the life of a country rustic. Haslam, however, persuades Jones to leave his preferred anonymity and rural life, to demonstrate his powers before the Bureau of Advanced Science in London. But there he makes a very dangerous enemy of Dr. Carfax . . .

JOHN RUSSELL FEARN

◆

MIRACLE MAN

Complete and Unabridged

LINFORD
Leicester

First published in Great Britain

First Linford Edition
published 2010

British Library CIP Data

Fearn, John Russell, *1908 – 1960.*
 Miracle man. - - (Linford mystery library)
 1. Miracle workers- -Fiction.
 2. Scientists- -Fiction. 3. Suspense fiction.
 4. Large type books.
 I. Title II. Series
 823.9'12–dc22

 ISBN 978–1–44480–067–8

Published by
F. A. Thorpe (Publishing)
Anstey, Leicestershire

Set by Words & Graphics Ltd.
Anstey, Leicestershire
Printed and bound in Great Britain by
T. J. International Ltd., Padstow, Cornwall

This book is printed on acid-free paper

1

Mind over matter

To be at the top of his profession as a physical scientist at the age of thirty-five was an accomplishment which Dr. Mark Haslam owed entirely to his own efforts. From earliest youth he had allowed nothing to baulk his endeavours, with the result that he had finally gained his Ph.D. and several other degrees besides.

But gratifying though these routine accomplishments were in themselves, they ranked as nothing compared to this particular day. He was to be made President of the Bureau of Advanced Science and lecture upon his discovery of disintegration and its application to basic forces. To the layman, dry stuff indeed, but to the profession a subject of absorbing interest. In this year of grace nobody had yet found the secret of pure disintegration. It might even change the face of the world.

Dr. Mark Haslam mused on these things as he drove his powerful Jaguar down the sunny country lanes. It was June — and June at its best — with the green of the fields and hedgerows, and the blue sky streaked with ribbon-like clouds, looking as though a gigantic but lazy painter had smeared a white paintbrush across it. So quiet was the car's engine that the silver song of a lark came clearly to Mark Haslam's ears as he drove steadily onwards.

His home was in Godalming, Surrey, and his destination was London. Behind him he had left a wife who cared little for science but everything for her husband; and ahead of him was the unparalleled honour of becoming President of the greatest natural scientific institution in the country.

Mark Haslam smiled to himself and hummed a tune. The world was bright and gay and the future brilliant. Years of mental toil were producing their dividend at last. Then the car sailed straight off the road and into the dry ditch bordering it.

He had not the slightest idea how it happened, but it seemed to him that the steering column behaved strangely, or else he took the corner too swiftly. Whatever the reason the car's bonnet lurched downwards and, though he himself was not in the least hurt, Mark Haslam found himself well and truly 'ditched'.

'Blast!' he declared frankly, and struggled awkwardly out of the up-ended car. Then, his feet sliding in the slippery grass, he stood and surveyed, hands on hips. Definitely nothing short of a breakdown crane could put him on the road again.

Muttering to himself, his immaculate suit dust and grass-stained, he scrambled up to the road and looked about him. Nothing. Just plain nothing. The hot afternoon sun, the lazy wind, that infernal lark chirruping its inside out, some confounded cattle lazing in the distance — and that was all. No garage in sight and nothing on the ribbon of road that went away over the shimmering horizon.

Nothing? Mark Haslam looked again. He narrowed his eyes, tilted his homburg hat over them, and focused into the blaze of sunlight. He had been mistaken. A solitary individual was approaching, perhaps half a mile away, and at this distance he appeared from his aimless walk and leisurely thwacking at the weeds bordering the road, to be either a rustic or a tramp.

'Not that he'll be any good,' Mark declared irritably. 'But he might know the nearest breakdown telephone.'

Whilst he waited for the languid unknown to catch up he examined the car again, finally locating the trouble. The steering wheel had become unbolted, probably through a defect in the metal. The accident could have been a lot worse. It could have happened in traffic, for instance.

So, at last, the wanderer in the sunlight came into clear view, dust curling about his heavy boots. He was wearing an old sports jacket, corduroy trousers, and had a battered haversack swinging from one shoulder. He looked around forty, with a genial, weather-beaten face very indifferently shaved, and a panama hat, much the

4

worse for wear, on the back of his black haired head.

'In trouble?' he inquired, pausing, and his voice revealed that for all his vagabond appearance he had refinement.

'What do you think?' Mark Haslam asked acidly.

'I think you are — definitely.'

Mark Haslam's sharply cut features revealed his annoyance as the tramp smiled blandly, surveying the up-ended car.

'Miss the edge?' the tramp asked, reflecting.

'No. Fault in the steering wheel. Where's the nearest patrol phone? I need help in a hurry. I've got to reach London for a special convention.'

'Tonight?'

'Exactly.'

'In that case, Dr. Haslam, I'd better see what I can do. The nearest patrol phone is three miles back — quite a way in this heat, and the nearest garage is a good deal further than that.'

The tramp eased his haversack from his shoulder and then plunged his hands in the pocket of his corduroys, still studying the Jaguar as he did so. Mark Haslam looked at him curiously.

'You know my name, apparently,' he said.

'Uh-huh. Seen you in the magazines occasionally. Go easy with that disintegration idea, though. It could be dangerous.'

'Thanks for the warning.' Haslam's voice was sardonic. That a no-account tramp should dare to criticize such a marvel as disintegration was nothing less than blasphemy.

Still the tramp stared at the Jaguar, a curiously abstracted look in his eyes. Finally Mark Haslam could tolerate it no longer.

'Look, there isn't much use in your just standing there, is there? I'd better get on my way to — '

Haslam stopped, and if somebody had put ten thousand volts through him he could not have had a bigger shock. For right before his starting eyes the Jaguar pulled itself backwards out of the ditch on to the road, as though some super-driver, quite invisible, were in control. It was not that the motor was running even though the wheels distinctly moved. The whole thing was, in truth, a complete miracle in broad daylight.

'I used the wrong formula to begin with,' the tramp apologized, grinning again. 'Seems it needed B formula to work this one. I thought C or D would have done it. Never mind, I got it. You'll find the steering is okay now.'

Haslam gulped. 'Will — will I?' he asked faintly.

'Surely. Try it.'

Utterly stupefied, he opened the side door and tested the steering wheel. It was perfectly in order. *Everything* was in order, as though he'd never driven into the ditch. Yet he had, for the gouge marks from the wheels were still there.

'Who the — what are you?' Mark Haslam gasped, turning sharply.

The tramp shrugged, returning his haversack to his shoulder.

'Just a wanderer, Dr. Haslam. Can't stay long in one place. Gets irksome. I like the fresh air, the wind, and the good clean earth.'

'But dammit, man, you're a magician!'

'Me? Not a bit of it. All a matter of control. Anyway, glad I put you right. See you again someday, maybe. And remember to go easy with that disintegration of yours. I still say it's dangerous.'

Utterly petrified, Haslam watched his benefactor turn on his heel and continue his ambling, slip-shod walk up the road, his hand thwacking the weeds as he went. He was singing now in a rich baritone, something about, 'The kiss of the sun for pardon, the song of the birds for mirth; you're nearer God's heart in a garden than anywhere else on earth.'

'Hey!' Mark Haslam yelled suddenly, coming back to life, and forgetting all about his professional dignity he chased down the road. The tramp paused, waiting for him to catch up.

'I didn't miss anything, did I?' he asked thinking.

'Miss anything! I want to know what you did — how you did it! It was a complete infraction of all known laws! I ought to know — as a physicist.'

'I suppose you ought,' the tramp

agreed, and the sunlight showed that he had humourously twinkling grey eyes. There was about him an inexplicable air of happiness as though nothing in the world mattered.

For the moment Mark Haslam had forgotten that he had an appointment in London. He had forgotten that he was a professional man at the highest peak conversing with a tramp in a dusty country lane. Only one thing mattered: the miracle of the ditched car.

'What's your name?' he asked abruptly.

'Esau Jones.'

'Sounds Biblical.'

'So I've been told. Just happened that my mother and father were very God-fearing folk. They had high hopes for me, bless 'em, so Esau I became. Welsh folk they were.'

'What,' Mark Haslam interrupted, 'did you do to make my car come back on the road?'

'Well now, that would take some explaining.'

'Are you telling me!'

'And you have an appointment. Why

don't you accept the thing for what it was and let it go at that? I got you out of a mess, and I was glad to do it.'

'Which means,' Haslam asked, 'that you don't want to explain it?'

Esau Jones scratched his whiskery chin.

'No, it isn't that. It's just that I don't think you'd grasp it if I did.'

'I am a physicist of the highest possible scientific attainment. I defy you to put forward a theory which I can't understand.'

Esau Jones smiled good-humouredly. 'All right, Dr. Haslam, if that's how you want it. How about joining me in some tea and sandwiches whilst we talk it over?'

'I assume you mean from your haversack?'

Esau Jones laughed.

'No. I would not dream of asking a man of your position to indulge in the kind of fare which suits me — cheese sandwiches and rather tepid old English beer. So tea and sandwiches it is.'

He nodded towards the field adjoining the lane and Haslam felt very much inclined to faint. It must be the heat of the sun or something, or else he had encountered a master-hypnotist; for there in the field, nicely placed on a spot where the grass was smoother than elsewhere, was a folding table and upon it, on a perfectly white cloth, a fully-laid tea in the true English style.

'I forgot,' Esau Jones said in regret. 'We need chairs, of course.'

He contemplated the setting for a moment and two chairs leapt into being like magic. Haslam mopped his streaming face.

'Let us dine,' Esau Jones smiled, and made an elaborate gesture.

Weak in the knees Haslam climbed the bank and settled himself, staring fixedly at piled-up sandwiches, variously made up of lettuce salads, meat paste, and tea in a silver pot, cream in a likewise silver jug, and spotless white china.

'This does my heart good,' Esau Jones commented, settling down and ridding himself of his haversack. 'Help yourself, Dr. Haslam. Plenty more where this came from.'

Haslam looked about him in bewilderment. Nothing but the empty fields, his not far distant car, and he and Esau Jones seated like characters in *Alice in Wonderland* at the Mad Hatter's tea party.

'Obviously,' Haslam said, taking a sandwich, 'I was knocked unconscious in the car and I'm dreaming all this. Obviously it couldn't happen.'

'Sugar?' Esau Jones asked, silver tongs poised.

'Er — yes, thanks. I said it obviously couldn't happen.'

'I think, Dr. Haslam, that a man of your scientific repute should not be so inclined to stress the word 'obviously'. In your capacity you should approach any seeming infraction of basic laws with an open mind.'

'But look what I'm asked to believe!' Haslam cried, his cup in mid-air. 'A fully-laid tea in an empty field, and a car yanked backwards out of a ditch by no known physical means. I *must* be either delirious or dreaming. It's the only answer.'

Esau Jones chuckled. 'I admire your

ostrich-like approach, sir. Since you can't credit it, you assume that these things aren't actually happening. That's sheer ignorance, much though I regret saying it.'

Haslam gave a bewildered stare, then with the look of a man hopelessly bogged down he miserably drank his tea. Esau Jones's smile widened as he sat at ease, eating sandwich after sandwich.

'First,' he said, 'let us get one or two things clear. I am not a natural magician — if such a thing exists; I am not a mystic from Tibet; and I am not from another world. I am an honest-to-goodness Welshman and I know everything there is to know.'

'You — what?' Haslam asked, incredulously.

'I know everything there is to know. I never learned it. Never read anything seriously in all of my life. I just *know*. It's a quality — a gift. There isn't a thing in this world I cannot do. And because of that I'm not particularly interested in doing any of them. Summing up. I am the living example of familiarity breeding contempt.'

'But this is impossible!' Haslam cried. 'A man who knows everything would be master of the world!'

'That's where you're wrong. It is the ignoramuses who want to be masters of the world. Wise men have no wish to be. To me, supreme happiness is to be found only in wandering from place to place, alone with my thoughts and the fresh air. This world is very lovely, Dr. Haslam.'

By slow degrees Haslam got a grip on himself.

'I refuse to believe,' he said deliberately, 'that any living man, or woman either, can have a complete grasp of everything, much less so without learning it. Why, even in my own experience, it has taken me twenty years of hard work to become what I am as a physicist.'

'Which is your hard luck,' Esau Jones sighed. 'I just know the answer to anything without having learned it. Music, the arts, any branch of science, medicine, whatever you care to name, I can practice to the fullest possible human degree. One does not deny the infant prodigy who conducts a cantata at the age of two. Why deny me?'

'Because it can't be done!' Haslam yelled, forgetting himself. Then he looked at the tea table and realized he was talking like an idiot. An apparent miracle *had* been done, right in front of him.

'And it isn't hypnotism,' Esau Jones added. 'I never tamper with the mind of an individual. I regard that as sacrosanct.'

Haslam drank some of his tea and then said deliberately:

'You said something about formulae — B, C, and D, or — something. What on earth did that mean? And you also said you'd explain. That's why we're having this tea, isn't it?'

'Yes — it certainly is. Well, it's all a matter of putting material objects where they belong and not where they choose to go.'

Haslam wrinkled his brow painfully.

'I mean,' Esau Jones elaborated, 'that in the case of your car you ran off the lane and into a ditch. You accepted that fact as unalterable. You, a living, thinking being with the power of thought to motivate you, actually tolerated the behaviour of a dumb, unreasoning mass of metal in the shape of your car. I came along and by the force of thought compelled that car to behave itself and return to the lane.'

'Now I *know* I'm dreaming,' Haslam whispered.

'Not at all. As a physicist you must admit that which science has always proclaimed — namely, that the power of thought is infinitely stronger than the power of matter. There are instruments in any up-to-date physical laboratory that prove it. From this fact has arisen that very loose phrase: 'The triumph of mind over matter.''

'Which is what it is?'

'I suppose so,' Esau Jones admitted, squinting into the sunlight. 'You see, nearly everybody makes the mistake of letting his thoughts remain uncontrolled. He does not realize, and has not trained himself to understand, that thought is always greater than that which does not think. That surely, is plain logic?'

'In theory, yes,' Haslam admitted. 'But physical laws say that — '

'Physical laws have nothing to do with it,' Esau Jones interrupted. 'The fact remains that thought is dominant. In that way, since everything material is made up of atoms, molecules, and what-have-you, it is plain that any object can be created, or dissipated. It is simply a matter of having the type of mind that can do it. One which thoroughly knows it is the dominator of material things.'

'Then what was all that formula business you spoke of?'

'Oh, that!' Esau Jones laughed and poured more tea. 'I have different formulae for different situations. The 'A' formula is for something really complicated, and 'D' for the simple jobs. The larger the problem the more thought-wave variants you have to move in order to set up the correct agitation to make molecules and atoms obey your will. It isn't anything uncanny, you know,' he went on seriously, as he saw Haslam's vacant stare. 'We've all of us got the power by very reason of the fact that we are capable of thinking and reasoning. But as far as I can make out I'm the only person who can do it without much effort. As I said I never learned it: it just is.'

Haslam said slowly: 'Do you mean to sit there and tell me you have this amazing gift — which you declare is latent in everybody else — and yet don't advertise the fact? Man alive, why don't you proclaim it from the housetops?'

'I did think of that once,' Esau Jones confessed. 'Then it occurred to me that I'd be pursued thereafter by every Tom, Dick and Harry wanting problems solved. I didn't like that possibility at all — and anyway it wouldn't be correct. Nobody is self-reliant if they have their problems solved for them. We can all do it if we want: why should I interfere?'

Mark Haslam ate two more sandwiches and had another cup of tea before he felt able to make further comment; and then it took the form of a question.

'Take accidents, Mr. Jones — my car, for instance. What made that happen? Why did the steering go wrong? You don't suppose it was thought-waves which did that, do you?'

'Certainly it was. Unthinking objects can't do a single thing of their own accord. They must have thought-waves at the back of them. Somewhere, Dr. Haslam, somebody thought for a moment of a car plunging into a ditch through a faulty steering wheel — and your car got the effect of that thought-wave. The source of the thought might have been anywhere in the world, or even on another planet altogether, for there is no limit to the range of thought.

'Rest assured,' Esau Jones finished, 'that the power of thought is the most omnipotent force in creation, which is why it behoves us to watch what we're thinking about.'

''As a man thinketh, so is he,'' Haslam mused.

'Exactly.'

There was a long silence, then with an effort Haslam dragged himself back to things mundane and glanced at his watch.

'I've spent the most inspiring thirty minutes I've ever known,' he said slowly, getting up. 'I suppose I can't persuade you to come to the city with me and explain some of your theories to my scientific colleagues?'

'Wild horses wouldn't drag me there,' Esau Jones smiled.

'Very well — but I give no promise to leave you alone. A man of your talents can't be left to wander the country lanes. The world has desperate need of you.'

Esau Jones did not answer, but he shook hands frankly enough. Puzzling things out to himself Haslam took his departure, sliding down the grass bank and then crossing to his car. Esau Jones watched him go. He still watched as the big Jaguar got on its way and went speeding like a black speck on the white line that led to the horizon.

Esau Jones picked up his haversack and slung it on his shoulder, then he glanced back at the remains of the tea. It disappeared — table, chairs, and crockery. Down to the last crumb. It was as if it had never been.

'The kiss of the sun for pardon,' Esau Jones sang, as he clambered down to the road; 'the song of the birds for mirth. You're nearer God's heart in a — '

He stopped, suddenly catching sight of something in the lane where Mark Haslam's car had been. Going up to it, Esau Jones discovered it was an expensive-looking brief-case, securely locked. He considered for a moment, surveying the emptiness, then the lock snapped open as he studied it. Seating himself in the grass. Esau Jones drew forth the papers from within and pondered them, particularly the wad of A4 sheets covered in equations that dealt exclusively with the new law of disintegration.

In all there were twenty A4 sheets, every one filled with abstruse mathematical and Euclidean postulations. Esau Jones read them through, then bundled them up and tossed them in the grass. In a matter of seconds they burst into flame and little charred bits of paper floated on the hot air like feathers.

'Better for you, Dr. Haslam, and perhaps the whole world,' Esau Jones reflected, as he studied the briefcase lock until it re-latched itself. 'There's danger in an idea like that — deadly danger. As for the briefcase, maybe I'd better keep it myself in case our friend comes dashing back.'

But Mark Haslam did not come dashing back — at least not at that moment. He was thinking of his lateness for one thing, and his amazing experience for another. He had not even noticed yet that his briefcase had fallen out of the car.

And, meantime, Esau Jones was strolling on his way in the opposite direction, no longer in bright sunlight for, with the coming of evening, there was an ominous sultry oppression in the air and a yellow haze in the sky. Far away to the east dark clouds had gathered to deepening purple.

'Mister! I say, mister!'

Esau Jones paused and turned, smiling as a little girl came hurrying after him. She was a leggy child of about eight years, her chestnut hair tousled and her cheap cotton frock long since outgrown. In one grubby hand she held a bunch of wilted daisies.

'Well, sweetheart?' Esau Jones asked, as she came up to him.

'Would you mind much, mister, if I walked home with you?' the child asked, her big brown eyes full of inquiry.

'Not at all, little one. Come along with me, by all means. But I'm not going home. In fact, between you and me, I haven't *got* a home.'

'I meant my own home,' the child explained gravely. 'That's it there — beyond the trees.'

She indicated a distant wayside hotel almost screened by an outcropping of elms and willows.

'And why should you wish to walk with me?' Esau Jones asked in surprise. 'Surely I'm not very good company for a little girl of your age?'

'Well, you see, you're big, 'n' I'm scared of thunder. So I thought if it started to thunder I'd have somebody big to cling to.'

Esau Jones glanced towards the east where the purple clouds were banked. There was a stillness upon the land. Beyond doubt a thunderstorm of considerable severity was in the making.

'Even my flowers are scared,' the child added sadly, holding up the forlorn bunch.

'Well, now,' Esau Jones said amiably, 'suppose we work a little magic, eh? Just hold my hand and close your eyes. Keep the flowers as you're holding them now — Right! Now, off we go.'

In complete confidence the child did as she was told for perhaps a dozen yards.

'Now look,' Esau Jones suggested, and with a cry of delight the child gazed at the freshly upstanding daisies in her fist. Then, gradually, she frowned.

'But — but what happened, mister? You didn't change them 'cos I hung on to them all the time.'

'Oh, they just revived,' Esau Jones chuckled. 'Maybe I'm your Uncle Esau, the mad magician — I wouldn't know. Ah, so this is the old homestead, is it?'

The child fled away from his grip and went running up the pathway of the old-world front garden of the wayside hotel.

'Mummy! Mummy, where are you? I've brought Uncle Esau and he's a magician. He made my flowers all new — '

Esau Jones stood surveying the scene, and liked it. The place was old-fashioned and the front garden heavy with roses and laid out with rustic tables in readiness for teas. But there was, withal, a certain air of poverty, as though everything had been thrown into the breach to keep the place going, and yet had failed.

Then the little girl's mother appeared. She was a good-looking, tired woman of perhaps thirty, scrupulously clean, but plainly overworked. Her blue eyes studied Esau Jones and his smiling countenance as she came down the pathway with the child playing around her.

'Good evening,' she said seriously. 'Hilda's just been telling me you saw her home. That was very kind of you. I hope it didn't take you out of your way.'

'Not at all, madam, and it would have been all the same if it had. I was able to do the little lady a service, which was most gratifying to me.'

'Service? Oh, you mean the storm that is blowing up? Yes, she does like company when there's thunder about. Just a child's fear, of course.'

'I was referring to her flowers,' Esau Jones explained, settling himself at one of the rustic tables. 'But no matter. Just so long as she is happy. Would I trespass on good nature if I asked for a glass of beer?'

'A pleasure — but you'd better come inside, hadn't you? There's thunder rumbling at this very moment.'

At the remark the child looked apprehensively at the darkened sky, then around her on the immovable stillness of the trees. Esau Jones watched her and then motioned.

'Come here, little lady,' he said, and put an arm about her slim shoulders as she came. 'Now, shall Uncle Esau try some more magic and tell the storm to go and make its noise somewhere else?'

'Yes,' the child urged eagerly, entirely confident.

'Really,' her mother said, irritated, 'I do not see any point in raising the child's hopes to no purpose, Mr. — ?'

'Esau Jones, madam, at your service.' He rose and bowed slightly, then reseated himself. 'And believe me, I have no intention of raising the little lady's hopes needlessly. Watch for yourselves.'

As Esau Jones muttered something

about 'Formula B' to himself, little Hilda and her mother surveyed the blackening heavens from which spots of rain were already falling — then to their surprise there came an unexpected breath of wind that set the leaves of the trees rustling swiftly. Overhead the density of cloud began to break and here and there a patch of blue appeared. From the west a golden shaft of sunlight came stabbing through the trees and seemed to aim directly at where Esau Jones was seated. He blinked and grinned.

'Good enough, youngster?' he asked, hugging the child — She winked at him gaily, and her fears relieved went singing down the pathway and out into the lane again.

'Don't be long, Hilda!' her mother called after her, and to Esau Jones she added, 'These summer holidays! They wear a child out. She'd be better at school.'

Esau Jones slipped his haversack from his shoulder and, legs stretched, was studying his dusty boots, and then the briefcase on the tabletop.

'The storm seems to have cleared,' the woman said, looking above her. 'Rather queer really.'

'Queer?'

'Well — it was rather sudden, wasn't it?'

'Prerogative of our English climate, madam.'

'And lucky for you Mr. Jones! It enabled you to keep your word to Hilda — but next time I shouldn't take such a fantastic risk with a child's faith. Anyway, I'll get your beer. You'll have it out here now the storm's cleared?'

'Yes — and please join me. In conversation if not in drink.'

The woman hesitated, then turned away up the path, surveying the clearing sky as she went. Many mysteries were buzzing around in her head as she drew the beer in the parlour and came outside again with a foaming glass of ale in her hand. She set it down on the table beside Esau and remained looking at him.

'How much?' he inquired.

'Nothing, Mr. Jones. Please consider it a return for showing Hilda a kindness.'

Esau Jones smiled. 'Very well. Do sit down, Mrs. — ?'

'Canbury. Rose Canbury.' She seated herself opposite him, her tired blue eyes searching the weather-beaten, good-natured face.

'Excellent ale,' Esau Jones observed. 'My one weakness, I'm afraid. I neither smoke nor swear, but beer in moderation I love. It breathes England, and summer-time.'

'I wish more people liked the ale,' Mrs. Canbury sighed. 'Believe it or not, Mr. Jones, you're the only customer I've had today. And in such glorious weather, too! This place is too far off the beaten track to be a paying proposition, I'm afraid.'

'Possibly,' Esau Jones admitted.

'I knew it at the time — ' The woman's hands were working somewhat convulsively on the tabletop. 'But Harry just talked me into it. Harry's anxious to marry me,' she added, with an apologetic glance. 'He's a house agent and he sold me this wayside place as a going concern.'

'In other words he sold you a pig-in-a-poke?'

'I'm afraid so. I'm not a very good businesswoman. But why should I bother you with my affairs? I'll leave you to your beer — '

'No, no, please!' Esau Jones motioned her to be seated again. 'I'm really very interested. Obviously then, you are a widow.'

'Yes. My husband died three years ago and with the insurance money I bought this.' Rose Canbury's hand jerked backwards.

'And this Harry individual gave you a raw deal?'

'I'm afraid so. Not much I can do about it, though. Harry's the possessive sort. He told me there'd be dozens of people coming past here in the summer, but I certainly haven't seen anything much and my savings are running out. In the end I'll have to capitulate and marry Harry or else starve. If I were by myself I'd have quit long ago and gone to London to find a job, but I've Hilda to think of.'

Esau Jones finished his beer, his quiet grey eyes on the tired young woman's face. The more he studied her the more he liked her. What irritation there was in her manner was plainly only the outcome of low spirits.

'Tell me, do you take guests here?' he asked. 'From the look of the place I'd say that you do.'

'Certainly! I can take up to twenty — but I never get any, so what's the use?'

Hilda came wandering back into the garden, grubbier than ever. She made straight for Esau Jones and his arm went about her shoulders.

'Mrs. Canbury, you are in a difficult position,' he said at length. 'With no one else about you can hardly accept a single male guest. But for that fact I myself would stay the night, but plainly it cannot be done. Have you nobody you can call upon to make things — right?'

'Not a soul.' Rose Canbury hesitated and glanced at the costly briefcase. 'Are you a lawyer on holiday?' she asked.

'No, madam. I'm just a happy wanderer trying to dispense cheerfulness where I can. Oh, the briefcase! It isn't mine. I found it in the lane and the

31

circumstances attaching to it led me to believe it is the property of one Mark Haslam, a well-known doctor of physics.'

'I've heard of him,' the woman said colourlessly; then she held out her hand to Hilda. 'Well, come on, dearest. Time you went to bed. By that time you'll have finished your drink, Mr. Jones.'

Esau Jones nodded, smiled at the affectionate kiss the child gave his stubbly cheek, and then relaxed and surveyed the quiet of the now cloudless evening. He drank more of his beer and then glanced up at the sound of footsteps. A tall, arrogant-looking man of early middle age came striding in at the gateway, and stopped dead as he saw Esau Jones.

'Good evening,' Esau Jones said amiably.

'A customer!' the newcomer exclaimed, astonished. 'I don't believe it!'

With that he strode on his way up the pathway and vanished in the doorway of the big, rambling old house. Esau Jones finished his drink leisurely, then got up and also strolled up the pathway. As he lounged into the wide but gloomy hall, hands in the pockets of his corduroys, he stood listening.

'And what do I find? A man lounging around drinking beer! I should think you didn't expect me to turn up, otherwise you'd have been more careful, and him, too!'

'Harry, for heaven's sake!' came the weary, protesting voice of Rose Canbury. 'I get just one customer, and the moment you see him you jump to idiotic conclusions! Go downstairs and wait for me, will you? I've got Hilda to bath — '

'Very well!' barked the voice of Harry. 'And hurry up!'

Esau Jones lounged across to the reception desk and mused for a moment.

'Formula D, I imagine,' he murmured, and then looked towards the broad staircase as Harry came hurrying down it. In fact he hurried far more than he intended, for abruptly the stair steps themselves straightened out into a ramp and Harry came whizzing down helplessly into the hall to crash on his face a few feet from the reception desk. Dazed and bruised he got slowly to his feet, staring back at the perfectly normal staircase.

'Take a tumble?' Esau Jones asked pleasantly, and was rewarded with a glare of steely grey eyes.

'You don't suppose I fell downstairs for fun, do you?' he demanded. 'And whilst I'm about it, what the blazes are you doing here? If you've got ideas about Mrs. Canbury you can forget them. In fact, the sooner you get out of here the better for you.'

'And suppose I don't wish to go?'

'In that case I'll make you.'

'I think not,' Esau Jones smiled. 'To be perfectly frank, Harry — and I don't want to know your surname — I've taken a distinct dislike to you. In fact, I have always had a dislike for men who bully women. If anybody is going, it's you.'

Esau Jones grinned and looked down at Harry's feet. Harry looked down, too, puzzled, then he started violently as he was heaved upwards by the sudden appearance of roller-skates strapped to his shoes. Instantly he swayed and twisted dangerously.

'Out!' Esau Jones commanded, and

delivered a terrific shove. Helplessly Harry shot across the hall, out of the front doorway, and crashed into the gravel pathway. Esau Jones did not leave it at that. He charged after him, heaved him up, and then pushed him, still swaying giddily on the roller skates, out into the lane.

'Now run!' Esau commanded — and the skates vanished.

Harry, wet with perspiration from exertion and surprise, staggered giddily as the skates went, his goggling eyes fixed on Esau Jones's face; then he swung round and pelted into the distance as fast as he could go, not so much because Esau Jones had ordered it but because he was convinced he had come up against the devil himself.

2

Surprise proposal

About ten minutes after he had lounged back into the hall Esau Jones beheld Rose Canbury descending the staircase. She looked about her in surprise as she came towards the reception desk.

'Where's — ' she began, then amended it. 'Have you seen a man here? Waiting for me?'

'If you mean the obnoxious Harry, Mrs. Canbury, he is heading south at maximum velocity, and I don't think he will ever come back. Forgive me if I've butted into something personal, but there was something about that man I didn't like.'

Rose looked bewildered. 'But how in the world did you get rid of him? He's big and tough.'

'True, but he went just the same. I overheard some of his remarks to you upstairs and I thought you were better rid of him.'

'Oh — Well, you're right. It's the biggest relief I've had for some time in one sense. Not in another. You see, if I don't marry him, I — '

'So you said earlier, madam.' Esau Jones strolled around for a moment or two in the gloom and then came to a stop. 'I would very much like to help you and the little lady,' he said.

'That's kind of you, Mr. Jones, but after all, our troubles are not yours.'

'I'd like to make them mine,' Esau Jones said seriously. 'I consider you are a most worthy young woman definitely caught up in the toils — ' He hesitated. 'For some time now I have believed that my life could be much improved by the presence of a woman. Forgive me if my logic is cock-eyed, but it seems that if you could contemplate marriage to such an odious being as Harry you might contemplate it with me.'

'What!' Rose exclaimed, blankly. 'Great heavens, you have hardly met me yet! No more than an hour.'

'Time is arbitrary, madam, and I am a man who makes up his mind quickly. For credentials on my character I offer you your own daughter. She takes to me — and no child takes to somebody who isn't to be trusted.'

'True,' Rose admitted, still taken aback. 'Hilda loathes Harry; that much I know — ' Whilst assembling her thoughts she lighted the oil lamps in the hall and Esau Jones stood watching her in the yellow glow. Finally she turned and faced him.

'I am not taking advantage because you are in a corner, Mrs. Canbury,' he added. 'I state unequivocally that I need a feminine partner in my life, and I believe you are that very partner — with little Hilda as a makeweight. I would not choose to have your companionship without the formality of marriage, of course, so that would have to come into it. I shall not in any other way thrust myself upon you.'

Rose sat down slowly. 'Mr. Jones, what an incredible man you are! You look like a tramp and talk like a college professor! If for a moment sheer desperation made me consider this offer of yours, what is there on your side for me to gain? Have you money?'

'All the money I need.'

'Your appearance belies it.'

'True, but as a roamer I hardly require Saville Row tailoring. I remain assured of my ability to provide everything needful.'

'It's too ridiculous,' Rose decided, getting to her feet again. 'Thank you all the same, Mr. Jones.'

He shrugged. 'So be it, madam — but in the words of the poem, 'I shall not pass this way again.' Thank you for your hospitality — and good night.'

He gave her a grave little bow and strolled towards the doorway. Crossing to the table in the garden in the twilight he picked up his haversack and briefcase, and then went on his way to the gateway. A voice suddenly called to him.

'Uncle Esau! Uncle Esau! Don't go 'way!'

'Night, little lady,' he called, waving his hand. 'Be a good girl to your mother — My God!' he finished in horror as, all of a sudden, the child overbalanced in her eagerness and came tumbling down the short, sloping roof.

'Formula C!' Esau Jones whispered, sweating — then he sighed in relief as the child dropped heavily on a softly sprung mattress.

In that moment Esau Jones had started something. Rose had heard the calling and seen the magical appearance of the mattress on the path. She hurried to the unharmed child and caught at her tightly, staring at Esau Jones as he came slowly back in the gloom.

'Where,' Rose asked faintly, 'did this mattress come from?'

'Which mattress?' Esau Jones asked, looking about him.

'That — ' Rose pointed with her free hand and then started. There was no sign of a mattress anywhere. Esau Jones moved his feet uncomfortably on the pathway.

'There *was* a mattress, mummy,' the child insisted. 'I know 'cos I fell on it. Uncle Esau put it there.'

'He couldn't have. He was too far

away.' Rose was very quiet for a moment, measuring an unfathomable mystery; then she said slowly, 'Would you come in again for a moment, Mr. Jones? I would like to get something absolutely clear — And you, young lady, are going right back to bed,' she added, sweeping the child up into her arms,

'No, mummy. I want to stay with Uncle Esau. Please!'

'Let her stay,' Esau Jones said, following Rose into the hall. 'After all, she's as mixed up in this as anybody.'

'Mixed up is right!'

Rose led the way straight through the hall and into a big, fairly comfortable living room at the back. After she had set the child down she lighted the oil lamps and then motioned to the easy chairs. Esau Jones sat, briefcase and haversack at his feet and Hilda jumping around him in her bare feet.

'Mr. Jones, I want an explanation,' Rose said deliberately. 'I'm a woman of average intelligence, I hope, and tonight I saw a miracle. But for the magical appearance of a mattress Hilda would have been gravely hurt. I refuse to admit there was no mattress there because I saw one, and Hilda knows she fell on one.'

'Yes, she did,' Esau Jones admitted, sighing. 'Let's call it a small example of my being able to provide everything needful.'

'But that was something uncanny, Mr. Jones! Uncanny! Though it saved Hilda I feel creepy all over when I think of it — ' Rose stopped suddenly and looked astonished. 'Great heavens, that thunderstorm this evening! Did you really have something to do with it dispersing?'

'He can make dead flowers stand up, too,' Hilda said proudly, who had been listening wide-eyed to the conversation. 'Uncle Esau made my daisies as fresh as when I picked them.'

'Well, Mr. Jones?' Rose asked deliberately, and again he looked uncomfortable.

'It's difficult to explain,' he said hesitantly. 'It's a sort of gift I've got. I can explain it easily enough to somebody with a trained scientific mind, but I wouldn't expect you to understand it.'

'At least give me the opportunity!'

'Very well then. It simply amounts to my having the power to make material objects obey me. Everything material is made up of atoms and molecules — that never varies — and they are utterly at the mercy of the higher power of mind-force. With the correct formula for a specific problem material objects are compelled to obey. Every human being is capable of exerting this power, but I can do it without effort — just as some people add up six columns of figures simultaneously or play complicated music without learning a note.'

Rose just gazed — not stupidly, but with deep interest.

'Like the man in H. G. Wells's *Man Who Worked Miracles?*' she asked. 'I read that as a schoolgirl.'

'There's a difference, Mrs. Canbury. Wells's hero simply had the power of creating miracles, without explanation. I know exactly why I do what I do and can explain it. It is scientific law manipulated by mental force, which any scientist will tell you is possible though none, so far, has practiced it.'

'And does this mysterious power make you able to cure things? Like illnesses?'

'I have never tried,' Esau Jones answered. 'Since human beings are also atoms and molecules I suppose it would operate perfectly, but I have made it a rule never to tamper with personalities. They are individuals, distinct in themselves, and I have no moral right to interfere with their physical set-up. I confine myself to things inanimate.'

Rose was still not staggered. She had a feminine receptivity and she knew what Esau said was the truth. A wonder man had walked right into her midst without any fanfare or blaring of trumpets. He could put matter formations exactly where he wanted and claimed no credit for it.

'And with this supreme gift you are content to roam around like a tramp and ask only for a woman for company?' Rose asked at length. 'You could have the world!'

'I know, but I don't want it. I prefer to be free and dispense happiness wherever I find trouble. I firmly believe all gifts

44

should be shared with the less fortunate, otherwise they wither and die.'

After a long reflection Rose said, 'Had you just told me all this in so many words I would not, of course, have believed any word of it. But because I have seen for myself I accept it without argument. I'll come with you, Mr. Jones, because I consider it my duty that I should. I am in a predicament and you need support, as best as I can give it. That combination of circumstances did not come about accidentally: of that I'm sure.'

Esau Jones went over to her and gripped her hand gently. 'You'll never regret it,' he said, his voice quiet. 'As to more practical matters, I suggest you leave here. It is a useless piece of property, anyway.'

'Can't you change the conditions?' Rose asked, surprised.

'I can, but I refuse to influence people. If I made this the finest hotel in the country — which I would not do since it is against the law of the land — we still would not be able to make people come here. No, something different is called for, and whilst we work out what it is I think we should take a wandering holiday. We'll stop at the first registrar we come to and legalize our union.'

Rose looked doubtful. 'A 'wandering holiday' sounds very vague, Mr. Jones — '

'The name is Esau,' he smiled. 'Indeed, with my peculiar gift I might even appropriate the famous phrase: 'He came, he saw, he conquered.' Or is that too much of a pun?'

'It will do for your trademark when the world in general acknowledges you,' Rose said seriously. 'For believe me, I am not entering this union lightly for what I can get out of it. You believe a gift should be shared with others, and yet you shun publicity. As your wife I will not tolerate that.'

'I shall cross that bridge when I come to it,' Esau Jones decided. 'Meanwhile, to answer your question: I wouldn't think of asking you to tramp around as I do. I meant a trailer caravan.'

'Oh? You have one?' Rose got to her feet.

'I shall have when we get outside.'

For the first time Rose laughed. She had forgotten for the moment that no material possession was barred to Esau Jones.

'Just pack whatever is necessary,' he advised. 'We will lock this place up and return at a later date to sell it when we are fully decided what to do. Agreed?'

'Agreed,' Rose smiled, and catching Hilda by the hand she hurried from the room.

* * *

It was about at this time that Mark Haslam was driving like a madman down the country lanes on his way from London, only one thought in his mind — to find the briefcase he had lost. He had not discovered it was missing until he had actually reached London and by that time it was necessary for him to appear at the Bureau of Advanced Science. This he had done and had been made President with due honour, but the address on disintegration had had to be postponed because of the total loss of his notes.

This was a very inauspicious beginning to his Presidency and his departure from the Bureau had been made with almost unseemly haste, so anxious was he to return to the spot where he was convinced the briefcase had been dropped. To his fellow scientists he had made no mention of Esau Jones, chiefly because in retrospect he could hardly credit that such events had ever happened. The most likely explanation was that he had fallen asleep at the wheel and dreamed about them.

So, headlight ablaze, he whizzed down the country lanes until at last he arrived at the vaguely familiar spot where his car had plunged into the ditch. The discovery of gouge marks from the car wheels shook him somewhat and brought a return of the incredulity he had experienced during the sunny hours. Then there *had* been such a person as Esau Jones with his astounding theory of mind over matter.

This, at the moment, was not Mark Haslam's concern, however. He must find that briefcase. So he went over the ground carefully, car headlights flooding the summer dusk and a small flashlight in his hand. When his search proved fruitless he felt himself becoming frantic. That lost formula was of superlative value — and apart from that, if it fell into the wrong hands it might be capable of deadly misuse.

Breathing hard, his homburg pushed to the back of his head, Mark Haslam returned to the roadway and looked about him. In the distance were the lights of cottages, inconceivably far away — and they were behind him. Ahead was the darkness of the countryside — in which direction Esau Jones had probably gone since he had started out that way before the amazing 'tea party'. 'And I suppose he'll be sleeping under a hayrick or in the midst of a palace created for his own special benefit in the midst of a turnip field,' Haslam sighed. 'Can but try; home lies that way, anyhow.'

Disconsolate, he returned to his car, re-started it, and drove onwards down the gloomy lane, but for all his alertness he failed to detect any sign of Esau Jones. Indeed the only thing he did see was a brand-new trailer-caravan, its windows discreetly curtained, and drawn by a powerful car. With a blaring of his horn he overtook and continued on his way, bound for Godalming and home, where he would have to think what came next.

Then, as if he had not enough on his mind already, more things began to happen to Mark Haslam. He had hardly overtaken the caravan and come into a clear stretch of lane before another caravan loomed up ahead. Once more he overtook, with some difficulty. And when a third one loomed up half a mile ahead he began to wonder if a convoy of them had been turned loose. The odd thing was they all seemed identical to each other and the same powerful make of car was doing the towing in every case. That was understandable, but that the present caravan and the one he had overtaken should both have the same registration number was beyond all possibility.

Haslam blinked as the headlight clearly revealed the number plate looming ahead, the identical number to the one he had noticed only half a mile back. But there was the odd thing! There were no lights on the road to his rear. The previous caravans had disappeared — and yet there were no side roads.

'No!' Haslam whispered, shutting his eyes tightly. 'No, it couldn't be! Not Esau Jones up to his tricks — '

Just in time he pulled up as the caravan ahead slewed a little to the right and blocked all means of overtaking. The caravan stopped moving, and so did Mark Haslam. He sat watching intently as in the glare of headlamps a familiar figure in corduroy trousers, panama hat on the back of his head, came ambling forward.

'Jones!' Haslam cried, jumping out into the lane. 'The very man I've been looking for!'

Esau Jones smiled. 'For a man who's looking for me you take an awful lot of stopping, Doc. I recognized your car as you got ahead of me the first time, so I put myself ahead of you — and again you overtook. However, this time I got you.'

'Put yourself ahead of me — ' Haslam repeated slowly, and gave himself a little shake. 'Oh, of course! Matter control

51

again, I suppose?'

'Naturally. It took Formula B to move all this lot in time and space, but it was interesting while it lasted. And I suppose you want that briefcase of yours?'

'Then you've got it?' Haslam gave a sigh of relief. 'Thank heaven! I've been nearly crazy since I discovered its loss.' His mind relieved, Haslam's attention travelled to the caravan. 'Nice turn-out,' he commented. 'Though I thought you preferred to walk under the open sky?'

'I do. This is for the comfort of the lady whom I'm making my wife tomorrow.'

'Oh!' Haslam looked somewhat astonished. 'Well, good luck to you, and I'll have my briefcase if you don't mind.'

'Pleasure.' Esau Jones hummed a song to himself and knocked on the caravan door. After a moment or two it opened and Rose appeared, clearly visible in the headlights in her dressing gown.

'Good evening, madam,' Haslam exclaimed, raising his hat. 'And my congratulations.'

'Dr. Haslam — Mrs. Canbury,' Esau Jones introduced, and added thoughtfully, 'widow. And now, Rose, if you'd please hand me that briefcase from the table in there.'

Rose did as she was asked and Haslam took the case gratefully.

'You'll find everything intact except the formula for disintegration,' Esau Jones said, and Haslam stared at him.

'But — but what in the world do you mean? This case has not even been opened. Lock isn't even touched.'

Esau Jones smiled and a startled looked crossed Haslam's face.

'Now wait a minute! Don't tell me you've been tampering! Look here, Mr. Jones, this gets beyond everything! Where's that formula of mine?'

'In ashes. I didn't like what I read — far too dangerous, as I said at first — so I allowed the formula to burst into flames.'

Instantly Haslam yanked out his keys, unfastened the case, and searched through it hurriedly in the glare of the lights. Rose and Esau watched him; then finally he looked up angrily.

'You realize this amounts to theft?' he

demanded. 'Don't you understand that you've destroyed a secret which it took me ten years and more to work out?'

'Better to have the secret destroyed than have the secret destroy you — '

His face grim, Haslam relocked the briefcase. 'I am aware, Mr. Jones, that you possess extraordinary powers, but for that very reason I would have thought that you would know where to exercise discretion. Destroying another man's work just because you don't happen to like it is narrow minded and unjust. Much though I regret it, I shall have to inform the police.'

Esau Jones's equanimity was quite undisturbed. 'That will not do you much good, Dr. Haslam, and well you know it. No police can ever interfere with me, and in any case you could not prove anything because the lock of your briefcase has not been tampered with. As to the formula, you can have it back.'

'You just told me it was burned!'

'The paper version, yes, but I read it through. I can repeat it in detail.'

'Ridiculous!' Haslam snorted. 'Twenty

pages of equations! It couldn't be done. I couldn't even do it myself and I wrote it all down.'

'Between you and me, Dr. Haslam, there is a great gulf,' Esau Jones replied. 'I repeat, you can have the formula repeated in full if you wish it, but I would much rather you did not. The proposition contained in it, that disintegration of matter would be limited to the particular area in dissolution, is entirely wrong. You'd find the business progressive and would probably destroy the world. However, rather than be called a thief and a criminal I will repeat the formula for you.'

There was a silence. Dr. Haslam stood pondering on what Esau had said; and Rose, still in the caravan doorway, looked vaguely from one man to the other. Behind her, in the caravan itself, little Hilda was fast asleep.

'When I talked with you this afternoon,' Haslam said presently, 'you completely refused, to come to the city. Are you still in that frame of mind?'

'Definitely! What good would it do me to come to London?'

'I was thinking of the good you could do other people. I do not ask you to do anything elaborate. I merely wish my fellow scientists to see that a man who understands everything really does exist. I believe you owe that much to your fellow men.'

'So do I,' Rose said, nodding vigorously.

'Once I'm in the city I'm lost,' Esau Jones declared. 'I would prove more of a nuisance than a help. No, I'm not coming, Dr. Haslam.'

'If you refuse an offer like this — a straight run to the attention of the most celebrated scientists of the day — I don't feel like continuing with our bargain, Esau,' Rose remarked, glancing at him. 'You may not see it, but your outlook is terribly selfish. Out here in the country very few things need putting right. It is in the city where there is corruption and vice.'

'None of which I would touch,' Esau Jones retorted. 'I still say I refuse to meddle with people. Inanimate objects, yes — but I will never interfere with human nature, no matter how bad or ill it may be. Now, Dr. Haslam, what about that formula? Shall I repeat it for you?'

'Not now. I would prefer you repeat it in London as a demonstration of your extraordinary brain.'

Esau Jones rubbed his whiskery chin doubtfully, but by no means misinterpreting the look Rose was giving him.

'I mean it,' she insisted. 'If I'm to become your wife I will not have you tramping country lanes, drinking beer, and altering this and that as the mood seizes you. Turn your powers to account. You said yourself you believe gifts are made to be shared.'

Esau Jones sighed. 'Very well. I will come to the city, Dr. Haslam, but I shall not remain there a moment longer than I have to. When and where do you expect me to arrive?'

'Be at the Bureau of Advanced Science in Kensington by six tomorrow evening. You will find a commissionaire on duty. Ask him to find me.'

'And your formula?'

'It is safe enough in your mind for the

moment — and if you should not comply with my wishes I shall always be able to trace you. A man of your accomplishments can hardly remain hidden. Good night, Mr. Jones. Madam — '

Haslam turned, re-entered his car, and then waited until Esau Jones had driven the caravan from its diagonal position on the road. The caravan door closed as Rose retreated within.

As he began to gather speed Esau Jones had the distinct impression that he was left without choice for the immediate future, for he did not intend to lose Rose and little Hilda whatever happened.

3

The examination

So at six o'clock the following evening there drew up in the private car park of the Bureau of Advanced Science a massive-engined car and a trailer caravan. From it Esau Jones and Rose, now his legal wife, alighted with Hilda, wearing her best frock and hair-ribbon for the occasion, behind them. Esau Jones himself was hatless, indifferently dressed, but scrupulously shaved. Certainly there was no air of distinction about him, as the look of the commissionaire at the gigantic doorway clearly evidenced.

'The name is Esau Jones,' the wonder man explained. 'I have an appointment with Dr. Mark Haslam.'

'Very well, sir,' the commissionaire responded, who though he had been informed of what to expect had hardly expected this. 'Kindly step into the anteroom and I will inform Dr. Haslam that you have arrived.'

Mark Haslam, once he came on the scene, soon had the situation in hand. Rose and little Hilda — with the strict injunction to keep quiet — were conducted to a front seat in the visitors' gallery whilst Esau Jones himself accompanied Haslam to the big rostrum whereon were already seated quite a number of men and women, all of them clearly stamped with the mark of the intellectual.

Feeling intensely uncomfortable, Esau Jones sat down, surveyed those around him, and then looked out into the great body of the hall. The place was packed to the doors, partly with the public itself and partly with scientific experts in every field of the profession.

'I hope,' Esau Jones whispered to Haslam, as he sat beside him, 'that all this isn't just for me!'

'Sorry to dash your hopes, Mr. Jones, but it is,' Haslam answered. 'You don't suppose I'm going to let a man like you disappear among the buttercups and daisies, do you? You'll be famous — and like it!'

Esau Jones mopped his weather-beaten face and then set his jaw stubbornly. He had evidently made up his mind about something even though he did not comment. He sat watching as Haslam got to his feet and, as President, addressed the now hushed assembly.

'My friends, there arises amongst us sometimes a phenomenal person who, by his genius, raises the human race a notch higher. Throughout our history men and women of such calibre have appeared and to them we owe our gratitude. That being so I must explain that I convened this special meeting for tonight to meet a new type of genius — a man who has the absolute mastery over all forms of matter. Mr. Esau Jones.'

Esau Jones got to his feet because there was nothing else he could do. Rather vaguely he stood gazing around him and waiting.

'Like all the truly great, Mr. Jones is modest,' Haslam smiled, exuding self-confidence. 'Give him the open fields and nobody to watch him and he will produce a genuine miracle. Here he is naturally diffident — but I am sure he will agree to some small demonstration to prove his power. Once he has done this I will explain his theory as he explained it to me.'

Dead silence dropped. Esau Jones made no move. His chin was obstinately set. Then at last Haslam cleared his throat.

'Mr. Jones, we are waiting. Some small demonstration, if you please.'

At that Esau Jones turned, his usually genial face grim.

'Dr. Haslam, I was not told when asked to come here that I was to be a kind of guinea-pig. I have not the least intention of exercising my gift for the benefit of a hall full of curiosity-seekers. I am here for one purpose only — to give you that formula which is rightfully yours. There my obligation ends.'

'But it doesn't!' Haslam protested. 'You are a phenomenon among men, and for that reason — '

'Shall I write the formula down or

repeat it to you?' Esau Jones asked, ignoring the protest.

Haslam compressed his lips. 'Aloud, if you please. The scientists present will write it down and those who are not scientists will be unable to comprehend it anyway. Proceed, please.'

'Very well. Taking A as the periodicity — ' and so Esau Jones went on speaking in a sing-song monotone, giving every figure, fraction, and equation in the twenty-page-long formula he had read. The silence was intense as scientists scribbled quickly in their notebooks. Haslam himself also noted everything down and now and again glanced up in wonder as exceptionally profound theses were expounded. So, at last, Esau Jones had finished and remained immovable before the storm of applause that greeted his effort.

'That being done,' he said quietly. 'I will take my departure, Dr. Haslam. I am afraid I'm not much of an indoor man.'

'Before you go,' Haslam said, 'let me make it clear to this audience that you only read the formula through once, and yet have not overlooked a single figure. Twenty closely packed sheets of A4, ladies and gentlemen! Even without a demonstration we must admit that Mr. Jones has an extraordinary power of mental retention.'

'I wouldn't call it that,' commented a scientist on the rostrum. 'It is simply an example of a photographic brain. Some people have them: see a thing once and they remember all the details. Certainly it does not elevate Mr. Jones into being a phenomenon.'

Esau Jones smiled. 'For those kind words, sir, many thanks,' he said. 'Now I must be going — but before I do I would issue one word of warning. Many of you here are scientists and therefore understand this formula of Dr. Haslam's. I understand it, too, because I know everything, but I foresee the greatest danger this world has ever known if you try to put that formula into practice.'

Another scientist on the rostrum got to his feet and strolled over to where Esau Jones was standing. He was a very tall, cynical-looking man with an irritating air of condescension.

'Mr. Jones, tell me,' he said. 'What are you in ordinary life? What is your trade or profession?'

'I am a wanderer, sir, nothing more.'

'Indeed — and you have the temerity to tell us, acknowledged leaders of science, that this formula is dangerous? Where is your authority for saying so?'

'The authority of understanding the laws of matter to the last degree. Because I knew the danger inherent in the formula I destroyed it when it accidentally fell into my hands. But since Dr. Haslam threatened criminal proceedings for my act I considered it my duty to give him back his property. If you are fools enough to wish to destroy the world don't say I didn't warn you. And don't come running to me for help, either!'

The scientist laughed scornfully. 'I cannot imagine anything less likely. Mr. Jones — ' Abruptly his attention switched to the obviously discomfited Haslam. 'Dr. Haslam, what was your exact purpose in bringing this — er — gentleman here? Surely not just to read out your formula and prove he has a photographic brain? If so you have wasted the time of every man and woman in this building.'

'I regret,' Haslam said sourly, 'that you should consider my disintegration formula a waste of time, Dr. Carfax.'

'Not the formula, Mr. President — that is exquisite, and you are to be congratulated. I merely question the method of presenting it.'

Haslam compressed his lips. Carfax eyed him loftily.

'I understood you to say, Mr. President, that this gentleman here possesses magical powers of matter-control, and that if asked he would prove it to us. Forgive us if we doubt the fact.'

Haslam moved quickly to where Esau Jones was standing, hand in pockets, moodily surveying the packed hall.

'Mr. Jones, please!' Haslam whispered. 'I'm in a spot. I promised these big shots a demonstration. It was the only way I could get all of them here in a body and hear my formula; I couldn't have managed it otherwise even if I am the new President. Maybe I did take too much on myself saying what you'd do, but don't let me down.'

Esau Jones shrugged. 'In future, Dr. Haslam, don't take a mighty accomplishment for granted!' He studied the young physicist's troubled face and then relaxed into a grin. 'Very well, if it will help you. I'll do something if only to put that long-nosed Carfax in his place.'

'Good! Good!' Haslam rubbed his hands in relief and faced the audience. 'Friends. I have persuaded Mr. Jones to demonstrate. He will do anything you ask.'

'How about asking him to leave?' Carfax suggested dryly, and basked in the cynical titter that greeted him.

Esau Jones narrowed one eye. 'Since neither of us likes each other. Dr. Carfax, how about *you* leaving?' he suggested.

'I?' The academic eyebrows rose. 'My dear sir!'

Possibly he would have said more, only at that moment the portion of platform he was standing upon completely gave way and he disappeared from sight. From somewhere there came a faint howl, which was immediately drowned out by the yells from the audience. Those on the rostrum sat gazing at the hole in the floor, only to blink incredulously as it abruptly vanished and the planks became normal.

'That Mr. Jones has chosen to exercise his levity in this matter is unfortunate,' Haslam apologized uneasily, thinking of the austere Carfax tangled up amidst brooms and buckets in the below-stage basement. 'However, perhaps something more scientific. Any suggestions?'

'Produce a Crookes tube!' somebody shouted — and it appeared and disappeared immediately.

'A typical power-house generator!'

That too came and went and Esau Jones stood casually watching the amazing manifestations of his thoughts. By the time he had performed his last demonstration half an hour had gone by, and the first man to congratulate him was none other than Dr. Carfax, smothered in dust, who had escaped from his 'lair' and seen the latter half of the performance.

'My heartiest congratulations, my dear sir!' he exclaimed. 'I forgive your little joke. Perhaps I deserved it — ' He swung to the audience. 'Beyond doubt, friends, Mr. Jones must be accepted into the ranks of scientists as the greatest authority on matter control ever known, and given an official appointment. You cannot refuse, Mr. Jones. It carries a salary yet to be determined by the Committee, but it will be a big one.'

'Sorry,' Esau Jones smiled. 'I've done all I'm going to and I'd be glad to be excused.'

Carfax looked as though he were listening to blasphemy.

'Excused?' he repeated blankly. 'Most certainly not! We scientists have got to determine whence comes your amazing power. We insist upon it!'

'Where do you expect to find it?' Esau Jones asked.

'In your brain, my dear sir, of course! I am willing to wager my entire professional reputation that you either have a double-brain — as some people have a double-stomach — or else it is that your brain is fully linked up, whereas nobody else's is.'

'Meaning, I take it, that the accepted 'blank' area of the brain, supposedly there for future evolution is, in my case, already developed?'

Carfax looked rather surprised. 'Yes. I would hardly have thought that a layman would know about that.'

'I am hardly a layman, Dr. Carfax. As I mentioned earlier, I know everything. And I do not intend to submit to any brain diagnosis, either. I want to get away from here.'

'Why?' Haslam asked. 'Surely, with your mastery over matter, you are willing to discuss with scientists?'

Esau Jones sighed. 'I'd probably enjoy it more if all of you were not so slow mentally. Frankly, I regard all this as most boring. Now, I really must be going — '

'Don't spoil the fun, Esau!' came Rose's voice from the front row of the gallery. 'Let them have their fling.'

Esau Jones hesitated on an about-turn to the door. For the moment he had forgotten all about Rose, and the dictatorial touch in her voice made him wonder for a fleeting instant if he had been so sensible after all in insisting on her life companionship.

'It will not take very long,' Dr. Carfax urged. 'We have the Reactor in the building.'

'Reactor?' Esau Jones repeated. 'I never heard of it, though I'll doubtless understand its complete principle the moment I see it.'

'On the lines of an oscillograph registering electricity,' Haslam explained, motioning to an attendant. 'This reads the vibrational power of a brain, the normal being a reading of fifty. Yours should be at least a hundred above that.'

'I hope,' Esau Jones smiled, 'you're not going to be too surprised.'

What he meant by that was not at all clear; nor did he explain further. He stood waiting and watching as a peculiar instrument like a horizontal enlarging camera was wheeled on to the rostrum upon rubber-tired discs. Carfax, looking immensely sure of himself again, set to work on the mysterious instrument's interior, finally fitting into position a ground glass screen. The non-scientific

71

part of the audience, fascinated by this display of inner secrets, remained awe-struck and gaping.

'If you would kindly be seated, Mr. Jones,' Carfax invited; and Esau Jones obeyed.

Immediately afterwards a faintly visible beam of orange-tinted light enshrined his head, and upon the screen in full view of everybody appeared a spraying of electric charges which rapidly died out. Carfax, looking vaguely puzzled, consulted the complicated meters with which the instrument was equipped.

'By all that's extraordinary!' he exclaimed, as Esau Jones stood up again.

'Something gone wrong?' Haslam asked, hurrying across to where Carfax stood thinking.

'Not exactly wrong: just that I'm puzzled. See the reading? Twelve! Which is equivalent to the reading of a child's brain of three years of age! It doesn't begin to make sense.'

'Surprising, isn't it?' Esau Jones grinned. 'I discovered long ago through X-rays that I have a brain much smaller than that of a normal man, and it isn't linked up in any way so that the full brain is used, either.'

'But it's impossible!' Haslam exclaimed. 'With the power you have it follows that your brain must be exceptionally large.'

'This instrument doesn't lie,' Dr. Carfax snapped. 'We must remember that, Dr. Haslam. Incredible though it is, Mr. Jones has the brain-size of a child. I shall never solve the mystery if I work on it for the rest of my life.'

'The answer's simpler than you think,' Esau Jones commented, then as he saw the questioning looks he added. 'Only I'm not going to tell what it is. Maybe it will dawn on you one day. Well, ladies and gentlemen, thank you for your reception, and now you really must excuse me.'

This time, before he could be involved any further, he fled for the door at the rear of the rostrum and then hurried down the corridor beyond. Somewhat breathless, he finally came into the main foyer, to behold Rose and Hilda just descending the stairs from the visitors' gallery.

'I think you should go right back in

there,' Rose stated flatly. 'Really, Esau, what kind of a man will scientists think you are? Running off like that!'

'I'm not concerned, m'dear, what they think. I need fresh air and the chance to think in peace. Come on.'

His mind was made up and he headed for the swing doors. This time, having glimpsed something of the miracles that had been performed in the hall, the commissionaire was civility itself. Not that Esau Jones noticed. He stole quickly into the street with Rose and Hilda hurrying beside him. Only when he had the car out of the parking space and was careering down the main streets of London towards the country once more did he begin to breathe freely again.

'Never any more!' he kept declaring. 'Never any more!'

'Why not?' Rose asked deliberately, eyeing him. 'Just what is wrong with being acclaimed the greatest exponent of matter-control who ever lived?'

'Nothing wrong with that of itself: it's the atmosphere these scientists exist in that gets me down. Overheated rooms, clogged air! I feel half-smothered. Don't ever ask me again to come to the city because I'll refuse.'

Rose reflected, gazing at the traffic ahead. Somehow she did not look quite the same Rose of the weary face who had been trying to run an off-trail hotel. There was a new determination in her eyes, a different set to her lips. In a word she looked as though she was just commencing to realize that she was married to a man who could be indispensable to her as the lamp had been to Aladdin.

'Where are you heading?' she asked presently, and Esau Jones glanced at her briefly.

'The country, of course. Where there's a bit of peace.'

'I'm not coming with you, Esau. Stop the car.'

'Now look, Rose, we — '

'Stop the car!' she insisted.

With a sigh Esau Jones complied. He drew well in to the side of the busy main road so the trailing caravan would not interfere with the traffic.

'Now, Esau, listen to me,' Rose said

deliberately. 'We haven't had the time to talk properly yet, everything being concentrated on you visiting that Bureau this evening — but it's time to get a few things straight. Hilda, go in the caravan and play.'

'But, mummy. I want to — '

'Do as you're told, dear.'

The child grimaced but obeyed nonetheless. When the caravan door had closed Rose spoke again.

'Didn't the formality of a honeymoon ever occur to you?' she asked, and Esau Jones shrugged.

'It did, but I hardly see the point. Our union is purely that of — convenience, of business. I need companionship and you need support. It ends there — doesn't it?'

'In a way; but I still think our marriage calls for some kind of celebration. Certainly we're not going to find it moping around in the countryside. I want you to get one thing clear, Esau: I detest the countryside! I was buried in it so long hoping for customers I could scream at the very sight of a tree.'

'Oh!' Esau Jones said, morose.

'Burying yourself in the country may be your idea of fun but it isn't mine — and I won't do it. We're going to stay here in the city and live on the fat of the land.'

'But. Rose — '

'Nothing to stop it, is there? You have the world at your feet, and if you won't take advantage of it, I shall. In fact, as your wife, I demand it!'

Esau Jones's expression changed a little as he sat looking at her. There was determination in every line of her face.

'I reminded you that I'd drag you out of yourself,' she said. 'I want the city, the bright lights, the companionship of people who amount to something. I've had more than my share of the other side. First thing you can do is create a home in London here, exquisite to the last degree, and furnish it completely.'

'Can't be done,' Esau Jones said moodily.

'What on earth do you mean? Nothing material can defy your will, or whatever it is you use.'

'I know that, but there are laws in the

land and I am scrupulously honest in obeying them. I even licensed this car and trailer though they came out of no known factory. If I created a town house I'd have to have planning permission for it, and that might take months. Besides, my application to create just a single house for our private use would probably be unsuccessful, anyway — '

'Then create a permission!'

'That would be criminal forgery, Rose.'

Rose beat a fist helplessly on her knee. 'Then — then create enough money to make some high official do something!'

'That would be double crime. Forgery again in the money, or counterfeiting anyway; and bribery concerning the official. Believe me, Rose, having infinite power over material things is far more difficult to exercise than you'd think. I know because I've worked it out.'

'Oh, this is preposterous!' Rose said angrily. 'Don't you realize you are above every other man and woman in the world? What do their laws count when you can annul every one of them?'

Esau Jones shook his head. 'Sorry,

Rosie. I'm an honest man, and considering the terrific power of the gift I possess it's just as well I am.'

Rose was having a hard struggle with herself to keep her temper.

'You said you'd provide for Hilda and me. How do you propose doing it if you won't exercise your gifts?'

'I propose to do it by setting up as a sort of general repairer. I'll undertake to put anything right that is wrong, provided it relates to something inorganic. Cars, planes, radios, television sets, even ocean liners — anything you wish. I shall charge a fee for the job and I ought to make a packet. That is legitimate business. There is no law to stop a man repairing a fault in the way he sees best.'

'And you think you can do that in the country?'

'I think so. I propose to get a permit to have a small repair factory erected: I think that would be allowed where a dwelling house wouldn't be. Most factories of the kind I mean are in the country now.'

'And you'll put all repairs right by your miracle act?'

'If you wish to call it that. There is no form of matter I do not understand, so I could easily do it. If I don't make enough money that way I could augment things, by painting masterpieces or going on a concert tour as a pianist. Only I don't want concerts. That would mean city life.'

Rose began to soften a little. 'Just how did you live before you met me? You couldn't do just roaming.'

'No. I did odd jobs in what must have seemed a miraculous fashion for various people — usually in the gardening line — and made a bit of money that way. Money I dare not create, Rose. It leads straight to jail.'

'But you could walk out of any jail on earth.'

'Yes, but I couldn't walk away from the stigma of being a criminal. I won't have it on my conscience — '

'M'm, I see. And about this proposed factory of yours. I suppose, once you'd got the license, you'd just create the place?'

'No. I'd earn enough money somehow to buy the materials in the ordinary way.

You must understand, Rose, that I cannot be a random element in the scheme of society. If I produce things that have no normal origin I upset the order of everything: there is an addition in the scheme of things that knocks economics and finance cockeyed. I won't be a party to it.'

'You have infinite power to produce the greatest factory on earth in the twinkling of an eye, and yet you consider the regulations! I'll never understand that, Esau! And anyway, what about this car and trailer? You didn't have any scruples about producing *them*!'

'Frankly, I've never had an easy moment since. I did it because it was the only way I could think of to whirl you away from desolation. Having done that I think they have served their purpose. When the authorities check back on the license I took out and discover I have a car and trailer which have no factory origin they'll think things — and by law I'm not allowed to have built them myself without a special permit.' Esau Jones grinned. 'Bet you never knew there were so many things a man mustn't do, eh?'

'This isn't funny, Esau!' Rose snapped. 'I refuse to part with our only home and means of transport!'

'None the less, it would be safer. The greater one's power the greater the need for honesty. I think Formula D should see us through.'

It did — in more senses than one. Rose abruptly found herself sitting in the roadway, with Esau Jones helping her to her feet. Dazed, a little distance away in the deepening twilight, Hilda was struggling up.

'Uncle Esau, what happened?' she cried, running up. 'Where did the car and trailer go?'

'Back where they came from, little lady.' Esau Jones put his arm about her.

Rose straightened her disordered clothes with fierce movements. 'And now what?' she snapped. 'Do we walk?'

'As far as the station, yes. I have enough cash to get us back to your hotel, and there we'll stop for the moment whilst I re-arrange my life — '

Rose did not say anything: she was quite beyond it. The way things looked to her at the moment she might just as well have married a tramp instead of a man who could have mastered the world!

4

Too clever to live

Even if Esau Jones himself was not particularly impressed by his uncanny powers, the scientists he had left in the Bureau certainly were — so much so that with the departure of the audience from the main body of the hall they retired to the big conference room to talk things over. And small wonder. They had seen with their own eyes a man who in half an hour had torn up every known scientific theory by the roots.

'The point I raise is this,' said Dr. Carfax, now right back in his normal cynical, academic mood. 'Is this man Esau Jones safe to have walking around?'

'Safe?' Dr. Haslam laughed. 'Couldn't be anybody safer, Carfax, believe me! All he wants to do is tramp the lanes and drink beer. He told me as much himself.'

'And because of that you believe him?'

'Why shouldn't I? I'm as good a judge of character as most people.'

'No doubt: but I refuse to believe that a man who can make every form of matter obey his thoughts will be content with just being a nobody. It isn't even logical. Do you realize,' Carfax continued, beating the polished table, 'that if he took it into his head, Esau Jones could dematerialize the Earth itself? Then where would we be?'

Another of the scientists laughed. 'Stop being fanciful, Carfax! Why the devil should Jones want to do that?'

'I insist it's a possibility. If he develops a grudge against humanity — as a lone wolf sometimes does — he might wipe out everything material. For that reason I think he should be put under restraint.'

Mark Haslam began to look alarmed. 'Take it easy, Carfax! The man only came tonight at all because I asked him. It cannot be repeated too often that he places no personal value on his gift. You saw what a job it was to make him demonstrate it. Left to himself I'm sure he'll do nothing alarming. Anyway, he's

85

married now and that should keep him occupied.'

'His marriage is the thing I fear,' Carfax said flatly, and the scientists looked surprised.

'I mean,' he continued, 'that he is now chained up — I use the word with vulgar looseness, my friends — to a perfectly ordinary woman. Unless that woman be a saint, which I don't think she is judging from her remark from the gallery, she'll never tolerate a man of Esau Jones's powers just idling his time away. She'll make him a power to be reckoned with, even against his will, just as women in the past have boosted a nobody to international dominance. That man can change the world and everything in it, and before he gets the remotest chance of doing so he ought to be stopped.'

'How?' Haslam asked bluntly. 'He'll walk out of any prison and dematerialize any chains. You can't hold him by any physical means.'

'And you can't nail him down mentally,' another man commented. 'That would demand hypnosis and I doubt if any living hypnotist, despite the apparent smallness of Jones's brain, could prove strong enough to break Jones's power. Nor could we use amplification because he'd cancel out the amplifier. He's an utterly free agent.'

'Not if he dies,' Carfax said quietly, and there was an aghast silence. Though known to be coldly calculating, Carfax had apparently taken a step too far.

'That's murder,' Haslam said, dismissing the subject — but Carfax brought him back to it.

'Very well, it's murder. Which do you prefer, gentlemen? A man who may one day murder the lot of us by destroying everything around us — or the removal of the man who could make that come about?'

Nobody else but Carfax would have dared to so callously bring up the subject.

'As a citizen, and therefore concerned for my fellow men and women, who cannot honestly visualize the terrible power of this man Jones, I think we would be justified in being rid of him.'

'Well I don't!' Haslam declared flatly.

'Whatever guise you put it in, Carfax, it's still murder and I won't be a party to it.'

'You would prefer to take a desperate chance?'

'Not at all. I just think you're making a mountain out of a molehill.'

Carfax became silent, evidently thinking the matter over carefully. He still remained abstracted as a fellow scientist brought up a question.

'Concerning this matter of his unusually small brain: how do you account for it? It's a complete contradiction. As for Jones's own comment that the answer is simpler than we think, I consider it an insult.'

'Personally. I don't consider that problem so difficult,' Haslam responded. 'It's not the size of a brain which counts, but the quality of it — and it is more or less agreed these days amongst our physical scientists that the wellspring of intellect is not actually in the brain itself, but that the brain is the medium through which it is produced — much the same as a radio set receives a station. Thought itself, to be explained, exists infinitely around us, otherwise there would never be enough of it to go round. Some brains, no matter what their size, have quality enough to interpret thought more freely than others. I think Esau Jones is such a man.'

'Which makes him more dangerous than ever,' Carfax decided.

Haslam rose to his feet. 'As President of this body, gentlemen, I must put it on record that I strongly deplore Dr. Carfax's suggestion and utterly dissociate myself from it. I have talked with Jones more than any of you and know him to be a simple man of very high ideals. There is nothing whatever to fear from him.'

Dr. Carfax shrugged. 'Very well then, for the moment let us forget him.' He gave certain of his colleagues a warning glance. 'Instead let us turn to more immediate matters — your formula, Dr. Haslam, for instance. Naturally you are going to arrange for a test?'

Feeling that he had won his point concerning Esau Jones, Mark Haslam seated himself again.

'I consider we should make an

experimental test tomorrow,' he replied. 'I have a model disintegration apparatus at home built exactly to scale — but of course it was no use without the formula of quantities which Esau Jones recounted from the original formula I made.'

'And there's another point,' Carfax remarked. 'Jones, without anybody's leave, and yours least of all, mentally photographed your entire formula and then destroyed your work. The fact that he revealed it again to you does not alter the issue — that he will commit a criminal act if he feels like so doing. However, please continue.'

'I'll not go into details of my disintegrator now,' Haslam continued. 'What I propose to do, after explaining its workings tomorrow, is annihilate a special substance which I call *infiniform*. It is composed of every known stable element in the Periodic Table. If that can be disintegrated, since all are included in it, it will prove the efficacy of my discovery. To create and fashion *infiniform* took me ten years, but I think every minute was worth it.'

'I take it,' Carfax asked, 'that you will

convene all scientists to be present?'

'Those who matter are in this room right now. I know that all of you are British and that scientists in other countries have not been invited, but that can come later. Let us satisfy ourselves first. If this disintegration principle of mine works, gentlemen, we have in our hands the greatest weapon of defence ever conceived — and I don't claim personal credit for it, either, since it is the outcome of many ideas expressed by differing scientists at various times.'

A fellow physicist at the far end of the table questioned: 'Why do you suppose Esau Jones was so emphatic in his warning not to try out the invention?'

'I cannot imagine,' Haslam replied. 'In any case he certainly cannot be allowed to hinder the development of science. The invention will be tested — tomorrow about noon. That agreeable, gentlemen?'

The others nodded, and at that Haslam got to his feet again.

'Thank you. And now I must be going. Quite a distance home and it's getting late. See you tomorrow.'

He took his departure quickly and one by one his immediate followers also began to leave. Finally there were only four men left in the big room, comfortably smoking their cigars. They were Dr. Carfax and three scientists who always more or less clung to him in all he said and did, chiefly because they owed influential scientific positions to his beneficence.

'Well, my friends, to revert to Jones,' Carfax said, his cynical face becoming grim. 'I was absolutely in earnest in everything I said. He's definitely a menace. Why, even the formula of disintegration is his property as well. With a brain like his he can write that formula down at any moment he chooses. A most useful gift to hand to an enemy of this country.'

Whether the three other scientists believed Esau Jones was quite so low as Carfax depicted they did not reveal. Such would not have been good policy.

'Yes, he must be attended to,' Carfax declared. 'I'll put a couple of good men on to his trail right away and let them handle it. If he has retired into the country all the better. Many queer things happen outside a city. The fact remains that Mr. Esau Jones is literally too clever to live.'

And at that moment the 'man too clever to live' was alighting with Rose and little Hilda from the train at Little Mereham station, half a mile from Rose's 'backwoods' hotel. Esau Jones himself was looking depressed, Rose was tight-lipped, and the child was cross with fatigue. The train had been hot and Rose was outspoken. It was pleasant to have the cool of the summer dusk and the lane to traverse.

'Possibly,' Esau Jones commented, as he carried the nearly sleeping Hilda in his arms, 'we made a mistake, Rosie, in our sudden decision to run our lives together. We don't seem to have done much else but quarrel ever since leaving the registrar's office. If you want to make an end to it before we get too deeply involved just say so. I'm willing.'

'I thought, you said you had to have a woman for companionship.'

'I did, yes, but not one who is eternally

going to pester me to do things I never intend to do. That way lies chaos and ill humour for both of us. Let it be understood, once and for all, that I will not step outside the law no matter how powerful the gift I possess.'

'Which means I might as well have married an ordinary man. I haven't the least advantage.'

'Your alternative was the unspeakable Harry, or so you said. Please don't forget that. And in time I will give you everything I promised, but I'll do it honestly.'

The gloomy hotel in the midst of the trees had been reached before Rose ventured comment again.

'I'm sorry, Esau.' she said quietly. 'Put it all down to me expecting too much. I realize that you're right.'

'That's a relief,' he commented, and waited whilst the girl opened the heavy front door.

Once Hilda had been put to bed Rose prepared a meagre supper from what few provisions there were left, and as far as Esau Jones could judge her manner had become entirely amenable again. What he did not, or else could not, realize was that Rose was in an extremely difficult position. She was only a human being, as the analytical Carfax had observed to his contemporaries, and besides possessing ordinary human failings she had the added one of a strong streak of avarice, arising out of her hardships in the hotel that had never paid. Thus, to have married a man with incredible gifts, only to find he would not use them except by honest means, had come as a shattering discovery. Her quietness at the moment was not so much because she had become amenable but because she wanted to think what came next.

'I suppose,' she asked, when the supper was nearly over, 'we start trying to sell this place tomorrow?'

'We do,' Esau Jones replied. 'And I'll attend to it. With the money — if you're agreeable — we can get the materials for that small factory I want, meanwhile living in a furnished cottage somewhere around here. That shouldn't be difficult.'

'All the world, and have to live in a

cottage,' she sighed. 'Oh well, what's the use of arguing?'

She did not pursue the subject and cleared away the supper things mainly in silence. Then with everything packed away she said:

'I'll sleep in Hilda's room for tonight in case she's restive after so much excitement. You can have number one guest room. Right?'

'Suits me,' Esau Jones responded — and fifteen minutes later he was settling in bed, wondering if it would be worth his while to turn the wind round to the east since the air was devilish hot.

He fell asleep debating this point, quite unaware that in the gloom of the summer night two men were concentrated on terminating his earthly existence. They were more than in the mood for it after the struggle they had tracing him.

Given all the details by Dr. Carfax they had picked up the thread of a caravan and trailer and then mysteriously lost it on one of the main London thoroughfares. But since this incident had been witnessed by the baffled proprietor of a corner shop he had volunteered information, describing the occurrence and pointing straight to the railway station. An alert booking clerk who had given the tickets to a weather-beaten man, accompanied by a woman and a little girl, was able to disclose their destination to the two men whom he fancied were from Scotland Yard.

So to Little Mereham where the trail had been easy. Knowing Rose Canbury well — he was unaware of her remarriage — the stationmaster of Little Mereham could think of only one place where she had gone, and that was the Elms Hotel. So now the two tired and determined men stood in the shadow of the trees and surveyed the gloomy pile.

'What do you suppose that shopkeeper was talking about, saying the car and trailer vanished into thin air?' one of them asked his companion. 'It had been seen up to that corner: we proved it. That newspaper seller saw it.'

'To hell with that. Probably the shopkeeper was crazy. I'm only hoping we got the right place now we're here. Looks stone dead to me. We'd better look around.'

This they did with practiced skill, making no sounds. Even so it was a full hour, and long past midnight, before their precarious surveys through the windows of the upper rooms brought them to the one they wanted. Dimly, as they used the tough ivy for support, they could descry the figure of Esau Jones as he lay in bed, blissfully asleep.

'Suppose that's him?' one of them whispered.

'Can't be anybody else. There's only that woman and the kid in the rest of the place: we've found that out. It's him all right. Let's get busy and deal with him.'

Carfax, evidently, could not run true even with his own followers, for he had given the men no hint of the fact that Esau Jones possessed supernormal powers — otherwise they would never have wormed into the bedroom with such confidence. And, once within, they took good care to leave the window open and silently glided towards the bed.

The taller of the two men pulled a gun,

fitted with a silencer, from under his coat and leveled it — then he turned sharply in alarm as something clattered from the dressing table. It was a small vase, caught by the in-streaming curtain, as the night wind stirred the oppressive heat.

Immediately Esau Jones opened his eyes, and looked straight into the dark muzzle of the gun's silencer and the two men looming behind it.

'Sorry, but this is it,' the gunman said. 'You Esau Jones?'

'I am.' Esau Jones forced himself to be fully awake in split seconds and in consequence the gunman suddenly found the silencer of his weapon bending into a graceful 'U'.

'What the hell — ' he whispered, panic-stricken; then rather than question defiance of natural laws he whirled round for the window with his startled companion right behind him. But, before they could scramble through it, inch-thick bars, firmly cemented, flashed into being over the opening. Utterly staggered, they fell back.

Light blazed in the bedroom — a

scintillating electric chandelier descending from the ceiling, even though there was no power laid on. Esau Jones calmly scrambled out of bed and then pulled on trousers and belted them. In fascinated silence the two men watched him.

'Now, gentlemen,' he said finally, 'what is all this about?'

'What it's about doesn't matter any more,' panted the one with the maltreated gun. 'The point is: who in Hades are *you*? How did this gun get like this? How did these bars get here?'

'That's my affair. And I want an answer to my question. Who sent you here? Obviously the object was to kill me had I not awakened when I did. By whose orders?'

Scared though they were neither man showed signs of answering the question. Esau Jones waited for a moment or two and then under his breath murmured something: 'Formula C.'

Instantly a complete circle of thin but immensely tough bars forming a cage sprang up around the men and a steel grid fitted exactly on the top. Terrified, they made frantic efforts to escape but it was quite impossible. They only desisted, perspiration pouring down their faces, as they realized the cage was slowly narrowing its area, forcing them closer and closer together whilst Esau Jones sat on the bed edge and watched.

'Entirely up to you, my friends,' he explained. 'Tell me the facts or be crushed to death. I have no pity for murderers, potential or actual. Nothing can stop that cage crushing you because it is not motivated by electric power, but by the illimitable power of mind control.'

'It's Old Nick himself!' the taller man shouted: 'Buck, we're sunk!'

Buck wasted no time in futile words: he spoke vital ones, and quickly.

'It was Dr. Carfax who sent us, Mr. Jones! That's the honest truth. We tracked you from London.'

The cage instantly vanished. Dazed, bruised with their efforts at escape, and definitely with all the fight gone out of them, the two men tottered forward. They clutched at the bed-end for support.

'Dr. Carfax, eh?' Esau Jones narrowed

one eye. 'I see. And his motive? Not because I played a trick on him this evening in the Science Bureau, surely?'

'All he said was you're dangerous and had got to be rubbed out. We don't know no more than that, Mr. Jones.'

'And Dr. Carfax gave you no hint as to the kind of man you would have to deal with?'

'None, mister! Believe me if he had we wouldn't have come. All else apart, how d'you do it?'

'That's no concern of yours. I — '

Esau Jones got to his feet at an urgent rapping on the door; then, since it was unlocked, Rose came hurrying in, a gown thrown hastily about her night attire.

'What in — ?' she began, and then stopped, gazing blankly at the two gunmen.

'We have visitors, Rosie,' Esau Jones said calmly. 'And but for a falling vase I'd now be a dead man.' And he briefly explained what had happened.

'I'll get my things on and go for the police whilst you keep them there,' she decided, and turned to go.

'No,' Esau Jones said — and in surprise she looked back at him.

'But they tried to murder you, Esau! You can't let them get away with that!'

'I can, and I shall, if only to show Dr. Carfax and his equally low-down associates, that I am completely immune from anything they can think up against me. Go on, you two,' Esau Jones added curtly. 'Get out — the way you came, and tell Dr. Carfax exactly what happened to you.'

The bars against the window disappeared and, shaken though they were, the two men hesitated no longer. Still convinced that they had met Lucifer face-to-face they scrambled out into the night and vanished.

Rose walked across the room and picked up the twisted gun and silencer. She gave Esau Jones a questioning look.

'The weapon of murder,' he explained. 'I thought my way out just in time. And all this is a decided shock,' he added, shaking his head. 'Presumably those scientists whom I did my best to please this evening plotted afterwards to encompass my destruction. Presumably also, Dr.

Haslam must have been amongst them. I wouldn't have thought it of Haslam.'

'One of these days you'll perhaps learn sense,' Rose said bitterly, throwing the gun on the dressing table. 'If you'd rid yourself of all these tomfool notions about honesty and hit back with all the power you've got you'd have nobody on earth willing to try and destroy you. It's the only way, Esau. A man with your gift has got to strike first to avoid being killed.'

'That takes thinking about,' he replied. 'I still cannot see that two blacks make a white. Anyway, Rosie, you're missing your rest. Better retire again, and don't worry about me.'

'Easier said than done, Esau,' she remarked, crossing to the door. 'You mean a tremendous lot in my life, and I still think you ought to protect yourself more than you do. I'll be alert for the slightest sound. It was that man shouting which brought me here.'

Esau Jones only smiled thoughtfully and with that Rose left him again and closed the door. When he got back into bed once more he lay thinking for a long time, pondering Rose's remarks and wondering if perhaps she was right and he wrong — but by the time morning had come, without the night bringing any-thing further untoward — he was satisfied that his own way of living was the right one.

'You are quite agreed that we sell up this place?' he asked, during breakfast.

'Quite,' Rose answered. 'Stebbins and Sykes, in Godalming, are the best people for the job. I believe Harry got it through them in the first place.'

'Which means we'll have to stay around here until somebody buys. I don't much like the idea of that, but it can't be helped. Meantime I'll see if the Authori-ties will grant me permission to build a small factory close to here. And you are also agreeable to whatever money we make from this place going to finance the factory?'

'Since you won't use the more obvious method I'll have to be. I don't notice you making any provision for us to live in the interval. I've hardly any money of my own left beyond small savings now that my widow's pension has stopped.'

Rose broke off at a sudden ringing of the main doorbell. Esau Jones frowned in wonder, then with a shrug he got to his feet and ambled through the hall. An official-looking individual in a bowler hat and mackintosh was standing in the porch-way, a briefcase in his right hand.

'Mr. Esau Jones?' he enquired.

'Right first time.'

'Ah! I'm from the licensing authorities. I'd like a word with you, please.'

'By all means.' Esau Jones waved a hand into the spacious hall, motioning his visitor to an oaken chair. He sat down, examined the interior of his briefcase, and finally brought to light a sheaf of official-looking documents.

'We'd like a little more information from you, Mr. Jones, concerning a new car and trailer caravan you recently licensed as new — '

'Er — yes,' Esau Jones said, and reflected.

'You gave your address as here, which is apparently in order, but the make of your car — the 'Conqueror' — is not listed in the trade manual. How do you account for that?'

Esau Jones plunged in with both feet. 'Only one answer. I built it myself.'

'And the trailer?' The official's eyes became needle-points.

'Yes. I'm rather good at that sort of thing. Nothing wrong with it, was there?'

'On the contrary, Mr. Jones, there was a good deal wrong with it. Unless of course you had a licence for your materials and your plans were approved by the appropriate Authorities.'

'Neither, I'm afraid.'

'So we suspected.' The official's lips became a white line as he put his papers back into the briefcase. 'I am afraid, Mr. Jones, you have broken the law to a considerable degree and you will hear further. Meantime the car and trailer are not to be used.'

'They won't be,' Esau Jones said dryly — and saw the official to the front door and outside. Rose, who had heard most of the conversation from the kitchen doorway, eyed her husband as he came back across the hall. The question she intended to ask was put by Hilda instead.

'What are you going to do now, Uncle Esau?'

'Yes, what?' Rose demanded. 'If this doesn't land you in jail, Esau, it will at least mean a heavy fine. Do you propose to sit down to it?'

'I'll answer that when I see what happens,' he replied. 'At least the incident proves that my policy is right. You can't do just as you like even if you have got infinite power over material things.'

'Ridiculous!' Rose snapped. 'Absolutely ridiculous!' and she flounced back into the kitchen to clear away the breakfast things.

'It certainly makes you think,' Esau Jones muttered to himself, wandering in to give Rose assistance.

She spoke but little until the washing up and clearing away was finished; then when Hilda had been packed off for a romp in the fields until dinnertime she turned to face her husband.

'You'll have to be going to Stebbins and Sykes, won't you?' she asked. 'Quite a distance to Godalming. Do you propose walking it?'

'Certainly. Do me good.'

Rose sighed and sat down. 'Then I'm not coming with you. If you'd created some kind of conveyance I'd have considered it, taking Hilda with us, but otherwise, no thank you. And the nearest 'bus route is four miles away.'

'You wouldn't expect me to create a conveyance after what has just happened, would you?'

'Yes, I would! I'd consider it the pointing finger — the absolute proof that you're a fool to try and live like an ordinary man when you're a natural-born wizard. For heaven's sake, Esau, come down to earth and see the thing in its proper light!'

'That's exactly what I am doing, and nothing is going to make me forsake my principles, Rose. Now it's time I was on my way to Godalming.'

5

Chain-reaction

Also at about this time the scientists convened by Dr. Mark Haslam were gathering in the main laboratory of the Bureau of Advanced Science. Mark Haslam himself was full of enthusiasm as he set up his model disintegrator equipment, but Dr. Carfax, leader of the scientists, was in an inexplicably gloomy mood. This was unusual. As a rule Carfax was fanatically impressed by anything in the scientific line.

'Anything the matter?' Haslam asked him, adjusting the beautifully made projector.

'No, no. At least not that you would understand. Just had some bad news, that's all.'

He did not add that it concerned Esau Jones: there was no point in giving Mark Haslam the chance to gloat.

'Now, gentlemen,' Haslam said finally, 'we come to the test. It may be epoch-making: it may be a flop. In practice I have not yet tried out my disintegration principle on *infiniform*, so it is the first time for me as well as for you. The projector works on the principle of projecting a violent agitating wavelength which, when it strikes the atomic make-up of matter, causes the balancing forces within all atoms to be destroyed. The collapse of the atomic set-up naturally causes the complete destruction of the matter concerned. Clear so far?'

The scientists nodded, completely satisfied with the theory even though it had never been practically demonstrated so far.

'And this is *infiniform*,' Haslam continued, and with a pair of insulated tongs he drew forth from a lead-lined container a chunk of greyish-looking metal. It had the appearance of anthracite, but was of obviously great weight.

'I gather it isn't safe to touch?' one of the scientists questioned.

'Of that I am not sure, but I do not

think it worth the risk. Remember, Gentlemen, that no metal like that ever existed in the world before. Every known element — barring a few unstable transuranic ones — is included in it, sometimes in a big quantity, sometimes only in grains or cubic capacity, as in the case of hydrogen and such like. I have devised it so that the gaseous qualities are imprisoned in the metallic content. Ten years of work went into it, and never once did I touch it by hand.'

The scientists looked at one another, brought face-to-face with something new in physics. If they had ever entertained any doubts about making Mark Haslam their President they were now banished.

'Now,' Haslam said, placing the queer substance on the testing bench within projector range. 'Are we ready?'

'Except for my secretary,' Carfax said, pressing a button. 'I wish her to take notes.'

There was a pause until Miss Amelia Barton entered. She was thirty-three, thin-nosed, mousy-haired, and knew science to the exclusion of all else — and yet on her left hand there was a diamond ring on the appropriate third finger.

'You are ready, Miss Barton?' Carfax asked briefly, and she gave a nod, settling at the nearby table with her notebook.

Haslam gave a final centreing to the model projector and then pressed the button. That which happened immediately afterwards was unbelievably violent for such a small-scale demonstration. The *infiniform* metal vanished in a blinding flash of light and the agitations it produced flung instruments in all directions, smashing the more delicate ones and flinging the unprepared scientists around like ninepins.

Haslam found himself flat on his face when the disturbance ceased. He got up slowly and looked around him, discovering his colleagues also scrambling to their feet, most of them disheveled but not one seriously hurt.

'What the devil happened?' one of them demanded. 'Surely you didn't expect an upheaval like that, Haslam?'

Haslam did not answer: instead he indicated the spot where the *infiniform* metal had been standing. Now there was a circle of utter blackness in the bench. At first sight it looked like a burn created by inconceivable heat and the scientists moved slowly towards it — then they suddenly stood stock-still, astounded.

The circle was not just a burn mark: it was emptiness. Total nothing and as black as interstellar space. No sound came from it, but there was not the least doubt that the hole in the metal bench was expanding very gradually, both outwards and downwards.

'What in — What is it?' said Carfax, and swung around to see Haslam's fascinated stare.

'I — I don't know.' He stumbled over his words. 'Hanged if I do! It looks as though the metal's burning or something.'

Haslam picked up a screwdriver and tossed it experimentally into the dark area. There was no sound — no anything, except that the screwdriver might never have been.

'I don't like it,' Carfax whispered, after a moment. 'Miss Barton, will you make a note of — ' He paused in surprise, noticing for the first time that the infallible Miss Barton was absent from her post. Her table had been overturned by the recent explosion and her notebook was some distance away on the floor. But she herself had vanished.

'Must have slipped out,' one of the scientists said, and turned his attention back to the slowly growing hole.

'She wouldn't. She's not the kind — ' Carfax was looking alarmed now. 'Come to think of it I didn't notice her anywhere after the explosion. Kemp, see if she's in the building, will you?'

Kemp, one of the younger scientists and an adherent of the great Carfax, did not like the assignment even though he obeyed it. He hurried from the laboratory and those remaining still watched the mystery spreading on the bench before their eyes.

'Definitely it's disintegration,' Haslam said at last, 'but in a form I never foresaw. It looks as if the composite metal I annihilated has transmitted its disintegration to the metal of the bench.'

'My God, don't say you've produced chain-reaction!' Carfax gasped in horror.

The scientists looked at one another in alarm. Chain-reaction meant the touching-off of atoms neighbouring each other, and it could be endless.

'Surely not,' Haslam whispered, but there was a doubt in his voice.

'Got to do something to stop this,' another of the scientists said quickly. 'What's the answer, Haslam? You have a neutralizing method for disintegration, I suppose?'

'How can I have?' Haslam snapped. 'That's like trying to put something back to normal after it's exploded. Only thing we can do is to get this bench outside quickly. Give me a hand. We'll try spraying water on it. That ought to short-circuit my electrical action.'

'Do that here,' Carfax said, and fled for the nearest fire bucket.

In a moment or two he was back, staggering under the bucket's weight and slopping water on the concrete floor. With Haslam's assistance he swung the bucket to and fro until at last the contents were swamped neatly into the hole.

Nothing happened. No fizzing, no steam, no reaction. The water just disappeared and the hole kept on gradually growing.

'I don't like this,' Carfax said anxiously, dumping the bucket beside him. 'It looks — '

He paused as Kemp came hurrying in. 'No sign of Miss Barton,' he announced. 'Nobody in the building's seen her.'

'She couldn't vanish into thin air!' Carfax protested; as the mystery of the hole obsessed him he added, 'Or could she? Anyhow, that must wait. Better get this bench outside, Haslam.'

Quickly the bench was swept clear of bottles and smashed equipment, then, held by either end, well away from the area of disturbance, it was carried out of the laboratory through the rear doorway and in the big flagged yard. The scientists set the bench down and then stood dubiously regarding it.

'I can't quite understand that hole,' Carfax said, frowning. 'It's utterly non-reflective, blacker than anything I've ever seen before. Wonder if it's gone right through the bench yet?'

In spite of the indignity he lay down flat, at a respectful distance, and peered at the hole. He saw a vision of the sky through it.

'Yes — right through,' he said, getting up again. 'In a while, at this rate, there'll be no bench left! It's chain-reaction all right, and you've got to think of a way of stopping it, Haslam.'

Haslam gave a distressed glance. 'How on earth can I, man? It's something that never happened before! Remember how we once said that atomic force would start a chain-reaction and that the whole earth would be dissolved? It didn't happen. The effect was localized; but here we've got it. And it's dangerous! Just as Esau Jones said it would be,' Haslam finished grimly.

'There's the answer!' Kemp exclaimed. 'Get Esau Jones on the job. He'll stop this in no time.'

'I'm against it,' Carfax declared emphatically. 'What sort of scientists are we if we have to call on that rustic magician to help us out? No! There's a scientific answer and we must find it — or at least you must, Haslam. In the meantime I'm going to look for Miss Barton.'

He hurried away, but whether he was really anxious to find Miss Barton or whether he wanted to escape the necessity for watching that mysteriously growing hole was hard to say. Whatever the answer, Haslam remained, still fascinated, the other scientists grouped about him.

Half an hour later Carfax returned, his search having proved fruitless, and he had no sooner arrived than the bench, eaten right through the centre, collapsed. Immediately, where the blackened edges struck the stone paving of the yard, more black spots appeared and rapidly flowed into one another, widening and traveling downwards.

'This can't go on,' Haslam said abruptly. 'We've got to try all the ordinary laboratory methods of stopping the trouble — and if that fails we'll ask Esau Jones. It's chain-reaction of a galloping kind, and it was probably caused by the original piece of annihilated substance being composed of everything that is known in the material setup.'

His face troubled, he headed back into the laboratory and surveyed the electrical equipment in an effort to decide what must be done next.

But, though a whole afternoon was spent in various experiments, the ever-growing hole in the yard, which had now soundlessly engulfed the remains of the steel bench, remained unchecked and was about two yards in diameter, pitch-black, and completely obliterating everything which was thrown into it or directed at it. By this time Haslam was one of the most worried men in the world.

Another worried man was Esau Jones as he made his way back to Little Mereham. Using what little spare cash he possessed he had made a trip from Godalming to London, with discouraging results. He wondered how he was going to tell Rose.

It was late evening when he arrived once more at the hotel. Rose had fixed up a supper of sorts, Hilda was in bed, and there was a look in Rose's eyes which made it plain she wondered where on earth Esau had been until this hour.

'Enjoy your ramble?' she inquired, when at length he settled down to the meal. 'Next time you take one perhaps you'll let me know. I found it tedious waiting for you to come back.'

'I haven't been wandering about. I've been in London — after seeing the agents in Godalming. I saw the Authorities and well and truly had my nose punched.'

'Meaning?'

'Meaning they won't grant me a license to erect a factory. I've got to prove the extent of my business and qualifications before being granted a permit, and naturally I've nothing to offer. I couldn't just tell them I make things obey me, could I?'

'You could have, only I suppose your highbrow principles would not let you.' Rose gave a disgusted look. 'And what about the estate agents? How far did you get with them?'

'I did quite well. They have a client who's looking for a good old hotel to convert into a rest home for the aged. The representative will be here tomorrow morning. I think we can call that a sure-fire sale. If so, we move out. There's a small cottage for sale between here and Godalming — Upper Newton to be exact — where we could be quite comfortable.'

'On what?' Rose asked deliberately. 'With no factory permitted what sort of living do you intend to make? I certainly don't agree to the idea of us living on whatever we make from the sale of this place.'

'I shall have to return to my former mode of existence and become an odd-job man, wandering around and making repairs as I discover them. It's good enough for us to get by.'

'For all the use your gift is to you, Esau, you might as well never have been given it. I'm afraid there's only one thing for it. The moment the sale of this place is completed I'm going on my way with Hilda. We'll have to arrange a divorce. The whole thing was too hurried between us. No wonder we made a mess of it.'

Esau Jones sighed. 'Which, interpreted, means that you only married me for the

Eldorado you thought you could get — '

'What else?' she demanded angrily. 'The whole thing was your idea anyway. We certainly didn't marry for love. It was a business arrangement, you wanted my companionship and I wanted your support. And what do I get? A cottage in the country bought with my own money, and you wandering about all day like a tramp, doing odd jobs! Using the greatest gift ever known for repairing broken-down cars and such. No, Esau, it won't do! If I can't be the wife of a wonder man, as I anticipated, then I wash my hands of everything. I don't consider it's selfish because ours is only a business partnership, and if you won't do your share as the partner, then I'm off.'

Esau Jones munched for a while and reflected, studying Rose's unhappy face.

'All right,' he said finally. 'If that's the way you want it. Seems to be no other course. Pretty obvious I was never cut out for married life. If this is a bluff to make me use my powers against my principles it won't work.'

That seemed to finish Rose completely.

She got to her feet, swept out of the room, and slammed the door. Presently Esau heard her in the bedroom overhead, and at length there was silence. He mused to himself in the twilight, indulging in one of those struggles that often came upon him when the temptation to use his power entirely for his own benefit was nearly overwhelming. He was no saint and probably would have yielded except for the fact that he knew how very soon laws and regulations could get him tied up.

And in far away London a problem of a different nature was still developing, and becoming more intense with every hour. Haslam, Carfax, and the rest of the scientists, all of them having hastily telephoned home to say they were indefinitely delayed by a scientific problem, were at the end of their resources to try and stop the seven-yard-wide hole which gaped blackly in the arc-lights trained on the laboratory yard. In fact there was not much of the yard left, and the main outer wall was threatened.

Haslam, as President of the Bureau, was the highest authority to whom anybody could turn — and he was utterly lost, and admitted it. Retiring into the laboratory to again consider the matter, he looked pale and harassed in the white lights.

'Gentlemen, that chain-reaction has been established is beyond cavil,' he said bitterly. 'Believe me, I never expected it, chiefly because such a thing has never happened before. It seems to me, from the reactions we've had from that growing black cavern of nothingness, that it is comprised of what Eddington would have called 'primal Universe stuff.' In other words, negative electrons. When the explosion happened a universe in miniature was present in the shape of my *infiniform* metal, in that it contained every known element in the Universe proper. The explosion *reversed* the process from which came our original Universe. In that instant matter was born through a primal explosion which brought protons into being to balance negative electrons — and so came matter.

'But in this instance we have an

implosion — the opposite of explosion — in which the terrific heat of the flashpoint stripped the atoms of all the various elements down to the basic negative shell-electrons — and that, according to Eddington, is the substance of which 'primal Universe stuff' is composed.'

'Yes, I think you're right,' Carfax conceded, after some thought. 'In that case it requires pure protons to re-establish the balance.'

'And to produce pure protons, stripped of all neutrons and so forth, is impossible,' Haslam said. 'That is where we face our difficulty, and nothing less than pure protons will do.'

A long silence ensued, filled with the thought of that hole outside, creeping, growing, expanding, silently devouring everything in its track.

'Well,' said Carfax finally, 'what's the answer, Haslam? If that hole isn't stopped everything in the world, and the world itself, will finally be dissolved into apparent nothing.'

'The only answer is Esau Jones,'

Haslam stated, and at that some of the scientists nodded promptly whilst others gave a dubious shake of their heads.

'I'm still against it!' Carfax declared, and set his jaw grimly. 'If we admit that Jones can do what we cannot, where shall we be? We'll make science the laughing-stock of the world.'

'Maybe — but if we don't we face the shattering alternative of having no world at all! It's the only way, gentlemen. It is obvious that Jones foresaw that this would happen, otherwise he wouldn't have issued such a solemn warning. That being so he probably will know how to stop the trouble. In fact, if his mastery over matter is as complete as it appears to be he should only have to will the hole to cease to exist, and it will do so.'

None of the scientists scoffed, for with their own eyes they had already had an example of what Esau Jones could do. But since that time the scene had altered a great deal as far as Carfax was concerned, of which of course Haslam was in complete ignorance.

'First thing in the morning — ' Haslam

broke off and stared blankly at the further wall of the laboratory. His expression was so odd that his brother scientists turned to follow the direction of his gaze, and like him they were seized with fascinated wonder.

For, despite the fact that the laboratory was securely locked to ensure the utmost privacy, another person had entered. She was a woman, curiously shadowy, like a being in a double-exposure photograph so that the laboratory fittings were visible through her body as she came forward.

'Great heavens, it's Miss Barton!' Carfax exclaimed.

'But — but what on earth has happened? Miss Barton, is it you?'

'Yes, Dr. Carfax.' The secretary's voice was clear enough even if her thin body was not. She had a ghostly appearance even at close quarters and her expression was profoundly troubled.

'How — how did you get in here?' Haslam faltered. 'Where have you been since the explosion?'

'I don't quite know, but to the best of my knowledge, since I understand physics pretty well, I'd say I've been in hyper-space.'

'Hyper-space?'

'Exactly. Somewhere between this plane of existence, and another that made no sense to me. It was intangible, grey, and contained no recognized object. I don't know how long I was there but gradually it faded and I found myself just outside this laboratory. Then it was that I discovered I had lost solidity in some strange way. Nothing formed a barrier to me. Even the very ground I'm walking on feels like sponge rubber, as though I'd fall through it at any moment. Otherwise I suppose I can consider myself unharmed.'

'Can you hold things and feel them?' Carfax asked, frowning.

'Yes, doctor — but only with difficulty. If I make a sudden effort I can pass my hand through an object, like this.'

With great care she picked up a pair of pliers from the bench with her right hand, then with quick movements she drove her left hand straight through them, back and forth.

'And that's the situation,' she said,

returning the pliers to the bench. 'I've noticed an extraordinary hole in the yard outside. What exactly is it?'

'Creeping doom,' Haslam muttered, 'unless we do something quickly. However, to revert to your own case, Miss Barton, would you come over here a moment?'

She obeyed immediately, as fascinated by her metamorphosis as were the scientists themselves.

Under Haslam's direction she stood in front of the electronic detector and waited passively whilst the instrument made a reading of her physical reactions. When he came to work out the mathematics involved Haslam frowned in wonder.

'Believe it or not, gentlemen,' he said, 'but Miss Barton's body has been affected in exactly the same way as my metal *infiniform*. She is composed entirely of pure electrons!'

Miss Barton started, but she did not look scared. Long trained in the mysteries of science she had learned never to be particularly frightened by anything.

'Is that — fatal?' she asked quietly.

'Can't think why it should be,' Haslam answered. 'Explained simply, it means that your physical make-up has been altered from electrons, protons, nuclei and so forth, to pure electrons. And that explains your semi-transparency and the fact that solids present so little resistance to you. You won't fall through the floor or the ground, Miss Barton, for the pure electrons still provide a slight resistance that will prevent that unfortunate circumstance. Whether or not you can derive consolation from the fact that you are unique in science, I don't know — but you are.'

'Being unique is of little use unless I can turn it to account,' Miss Barton answered. 'And, if I may say so, I am extremely hungry and thirsty. Do you suppose I can take nourishment?'

'You'll have to try,' Carfax said. 'Obviously you cannot be allowed to die.'

He rang the bell for the night-porter and before very long sandwiches and tea had been brought in for the luckless Miss Barton. To her intense relief she found eating and drinking quite as normal a process as of yore — so whilst she refreshed herself the scientists gathered in a corner to discuss this unexpected ramification of their experiment with 'Universe-stuff'. When at last their various conclusions had been pooled Haslam made a statement.

'Miss Barton, you have mentioned that ever-widening hole out in the yard. I think you should know that the only thing that can stop it is pure protons, and those we cannot achieve in the present light of science. But it also remains possible that, if we could but get a more accurate picture of the Hole, from an observer with a trained scientific mind like yours, we might be able to devise a method of neutralization simpler than pure protons. To state the matter simply: would you be prepared to explore the inside of that Hole and report back to us?'

'Do you believe I could?'

'Definitely, because by a fluke of physics you have become identical to the Hole in formation. If any of us tried it we'd be instantly destroyed, but you are pure electrons, and so is the Hole. I would not ask you to do it if I were not sure there is no danger.'

'Very well,' Miss Barton said, finishing the sandwiches. 'Since my main object is to serve the ends of science I look upon this as a supreme opportunity. But how do I get into the Hole? Even more problematical, how do I get out? By this time it will be deep, won't it?'

'As near as we can estimate it shouldn't be more than four feet deep. Whatever you do will be without aid of any sort in the way of ladders or similar articles, because they too would be consumed — '

'I'll do my best,' the secretary said, rising. 'And I am also puzzled by another point. Regarding these clothes I am wearing. They have undergone the same metamorphosis as I have. What happens when I change to different attire?'

The scientists considered, looking at the worried Haslam for inspiration.

'Ordinary clothes may be consumed and fall apart,' he said finally. 'Experiment for yourself at home and see what happens. If you can't wear normal clothes then you'll have to continue with what you have until we can solve how to restore your normalcy.'

'Just how did I get like this anyway, and yet none of you gentlemen were affected?'

'As yet I don't know the answer to that,' Haslam replied. 'Later, maybe, we will. Now, if I may prevail upon you? Time is short and the Hole is ever-growing.'

A general movement was made towards the rear yard, and the scientists looked at each other significantly in the glare of the arc lights. The Hole had extended to such an extent that it was now menacing the main outer wall of the laboratory.

'What exactly is it?' Miss Barton asked, staring at it fixedly. 'It looks like plain nothing.'

'It's 'Universe-stuff', as Eddington would call it,' Haslam answered, and gave a brief résumé of his theory concerning it. 'I'm fully aware of what you are being asked to do, and that blackness in there does look pretty terrifying. Maybe you'd prefer not to — '

'Not at all. I said I'd explore, and I will.

But first let me make an experiment.'

She went down on her knees on the very edge of the abyss, the scientists watching uneasily. For a long time she hesitated, then apparently struck by a happy inspiration she took the belt from about her dress and dangled it in the black void. The belt remained normal, showing no disposition to disappear.

'That proves your point, Dr. Haslam,' she said, glancing up. 'Pure electrons within a pure electronic area come to no harm, and since my body is affected in identically the same way as the clothes I'm wearing I ought to be safe.'

Having satisfied herself on this point she plunged her hand over the edge of the Hole, and still nothing happened. She was unscathed.

'Unfortunately we dare not help you,' Haslam said. 'You must take the full risk of getting in and getting out.'

Whatever else the mousy Miss Barton lacked it was not courage. She eased herself over the rim of the Hole, but it was not necessary for her to hang by her fingers and then drop. The hole was apparently only about four feet deep for her head and shoulders remained above it when her feet struck bottom.

She began moving, presenting a weird picture, as though she floated in absolute blackness. Realizing she was quite safe, even though sinking lower as the Hole enlarged downwards, she did not hurry her exploration. It was minute and thorough — and fifteen minutes later she clambered out again. The transparency of her form still remained but her expression was clear enough. It was one of regret.

'Sorry, gentlemen, but there's little I can tell you,' she said. 'You may not believe it, but the light from these arcs, though shining right on to the walls of this Hole, does not illuminate them in the least. It was like feeling at solidified Night down there. And since instruments can't survive there either I don't know the answer.'

'But the Hole is definitely growing downwards as well as outwards?' Haslam asked.

'Most certainly — and with extreme rapidity.'

Haslam sighed. 'Gentlemen, we've done all we can do with this problem. Tomorrow morning we'll get Esau Jones and see if he can help us. For the time being we'd better get home. We can't worry forever without relaxation. I'll give instructions for the laboratory to be cleared of all valuable equipment since it seems pretty obvious that it will be wholly or partially destroyed by morning. You, Miss Barton, had better take a staff car home, then no attention will be drawn to your peculiar appearance. Be here first thing in the morning, please.'

6

De-creation

At breakfast the following morning Esau Jones found that Rose had not in any wise altered her decision to leave him — so he calmly accepted the matter. Little Hilda, not knowing which to believe, was left in a state of profound indecision and refused to eat in consequence.

'But you must,' Esau Jones insisted. 'How do you expect to grow up big and strong if you don't eat?'

The child shook her head stubbornly. 'I'm not eating until you and mummy say you'll stop together.'

Rose eyed her. 'Hilda, don't be so ridiculous! Get on with your breakfast this instant!'

But Hilda only shook her head and sat back with her arms folded.

'Over to you, Rosie,' Esau Jones said, shrugging. 'The idea of parting wasn't mine, so perhaps you can sort it out. You don't want a starving child on your hands, do you?'

What Rose would have said was not discovered for at that moment the front doorbell rang. As usual Esau Jones answered it and beheld Lionel Stebbins, of the estate agent's, accompanied by a broad-shouldered, prosperous-looking individual with the stamp of officialdom about him.

'My client, Mr. Jones,' Stebbins explained, and stepped inside — and from that, moment for the next half-hour neither Rose, Hilda, or Esau Jones had a chance to say anything further. But, since the whole business ended with the client writing a cheque for the purchase price of the property, Rose's mood changed considerably.

So at last she and Esau Jones were together again in the hall, the still unrepentant Hilda lingering watchfully in the doorway of the main lounge.

'Well, that should fix you up nicely, Rosie,' Esau Jones smiled. 'Not a fortune, but then this is bad property. It'll keep you and your little lady comfortable for a long time to come, anyway. Glad I managed to swing that much for you, at least. Oh, Hilda!' he added, catching sight of her. 'Run and fetch my haversack for me, will you? And my panama hat. There's nothing else I need.'

'No, I won't,' Hilda replied flatly.

'Very well,' Esau Jones sighed. 'I can use Formula D just as easily.' And almost instantly the haversack and panama appeared in his hands. He considered them and then looked at Rose's serious face.

'That little cottage in Upper Newton should suit you fine,' he added, smiling. 'You know where Upper Newton is?'

Rose nodded slowly. 'Right, then. Nothing more I can do. I'll be on my way and what communications there are regarding the divorce can be sent to the post office in Little Mereham. I'll make it my business to call there for mail. 'Bye, Rosie. Pity it didn't work out better. 'Bye, little lady.'

He caught Hilda up in his arms as she came rushing towards him. She was weeping copiously.

'Uncle Esau, I'm coming with you. Where you — you go I want to go, too.'

'I'd love it, little lady, but it can't be done. You must stay with your mummy and look after her.' He set her down. 'That's your job, Hilda, and see you stick to it.'

'But I — '

A hammering at the front door, followed by the pealing of the bell, interrupted the child. Esau Jones frowned, then went to the door and opened it. He had hardly done so before he was touched on the arm with a long blue envelope, which was then formally handed to him.

'With the compliments of Denbury and Bayne,' said the individual in striped trousers and black jacket, and with that he departed.

Puzzled, Esau Jones came back into the hall, leaving the door open and contemplating the envelope. Rose, from sheer curiosity, joined him. Together, little Hilda trying to discover what was going on, they surveyed the folded blue sheet that Esau Jones brought to light

141

from the envelope.

' . . . Ministry versus Esau Jones, in the Court of Summary Jurisdiction . . . ' Rose stopped in horror. 'Good heavens, Esau, it's a summons!'

'Uh-huh,' he agreed, and then winced at the packed wording which summoned him to the magistrate's court for having created an article, to wit a motor car, without due reference to the law of licensing whereby . . . and so on,

'When?' Rose asked anxiously.

'Er — Tomorrow in Godalming. Ah, me!' Esau Jones thrust the summons in his pocket and turned to the door again. 'I'll go, as they ask. So, once again, Rosie, I'll say goodbye — '

'No, Esau, wait a moment! I don't want it this way. I've been in the wrong. I can see it all now.'

'Can you?' Esau Jones looked surprised. 'It's taken a long time, Rosie, hasn't it? Don't you think it's about time you made up your mind? You can't go on switching your affection like an electric light, you know.'

'I've been very selfish,' Rose said

worriedly. 'Maybe because I was afraid we wouldn't make our way. But now — well, I just can't leave you to face this court case all by yourself. I did marry you after all, and that includes everything that goes with it. Stay, at least until this court case is over. Besides, I wouldn't be able to control Hilda if you went.'

'I see. You must keep me if only for Hilda's sake? Well, there it is. Just another example of mother-love, I suppose, and therefore — '

'Ah, Mr. Jones!'

Both Rose and Esau Jones swung in surprise as an immaculate figure entered through the front doorway, removing his hat.

'Dr. Haslam!' Rose exclaimed, surprised.

'Yes, Mrs. Jones.' Haslam came forward and shook hands. 'I hope I'm not intruding, walking in like this?'

'Quite welcome,' Esau Jones replied. 'Matter of fact we don't own this place any longer — or at least my wife doesn't. Sold only this morning. We may be here for a while yet, though, and — But that doesn't matter. What brings you here?'

'Grim business. I'm desperately in need of your help. In fact all of us scientists are.'

'Oh?' Esau Jones raised an eyebrow. 'Carry on talking, doctor.'

Haslam hesitated, vaguely astonished that he had not been asked in the lounge. Nor could he quite understand the grim set of Esau Jones's mouth or the hard look in Rose's eyes.

'Er — it concerns an experiment we've made.' Haslam cleared his throat. 'We've run into trouble and we can't find a way to solve it. You, with your extraordinary grasp of matter-control, probably can.'

'On what terms?' Rose asked. 'My husband does no work without an appropriate return.'

Esau Jones looked at her in surprise. Her sudden decision to assume the mantle of business manager was a new one.

'You can name whatever figure you wish, Mr. Jones, but I beg of you to come back to London with me at once.'

'Sorry. Once was enough. And why not

come into the open, Dr. Haslam, and say that you experimented with your disintegration principle and now find you've made a tragic mistake.'

'Who told you?' Haslam asked, irritated.

'Nobody. To me it's self-evident. There are no normal problems which science can't solve, so it must be a particularly big one — something new. That means your formula. Against my advice you tried it out, eh?'

'I had to,' Haslam replied. 'None of the scientists gave a hoot for your warning because you're not an accepted scientist, anyway. Forget all that, man, and come back to London with me. We've got chain-reaction and can't stop it. During the night an entire laboratory has been destroyed. Before long the whole Bureau of Advanced Science will go, too.'

'That's too bad,' Esau Jones said, shrugging. 'I'm not coming.'

'But, Mr. Jones, this matter doesn't just concern *me* any longer. It's a threat to everybody. It's got to be stopped! I can't understand your uncompromising attitude. I rather thought we saw eye-to-eye in most things, even if I didn't heed your warning.'

'We saw eye-to-eye until you and the rest of your fine-feathered friends tried to murder me! Curiously enough, I've a strong objection to being murdered and I haven't forgotten the attempt that was made.'

Haslam looked bewildered. 'But — but I don't understand.'

'Or, more correctly, you don't wish to. Naturally I don't expect you to admit yourself a party to a conspiracy to kill me.'

Haslam stood thinking for a moment, then his expression slowly changed. 'I think I know who's at the back of this, Mr. Jones — Dr. Carfax. The other evening, after your demonstration, he conceived the idea that you are a dangerous man and said something about getting rid of you. I thought I'd talked him out of such a ghastly idea — and you say an attempt on your life was made?'

'My wife will verify it.'

'Quite correct,' Rose said bitterly. 'And I don't see how you, as President of the

Bureau, Dr. Haslam, could have no possible knowledge of it.'

'In other words,' Esau Jones said, 'good morning, Dr. Haslam.'

'Mr. Jones, for the last time — '

'Good morning, Dr. Haslam.'

Haslam compressed his lips, and then with a despairing glance he turned on his heel and departed through the front doorway. In another moment there was the sound of his car driving away.

'He's got his gall,' Esau Jones muttered. 'Seems to me these city folk will do anything just as long as they get their own ends served.'

'You're not going to let it stay like this, though, are you?' Rose asked.

'Most certainly I am!'

'But that's silly. You've let him know what you think about him. That being so I should do as he asks, say later in the day. You heard what he said. You can name your own price for the problem, whatever it is.'

'Do a job for those who tried to murder me? Not I!'

'But look, Esau — and don't think I'm

saying this to be awkward, either — you can really make a pile of money this time and still stick to your principles. Charge Haslam the limit for solving this problem of his. That way you can also get your own back on those scientists for their attempt to get you out of the way.'

Esau Jones began to smile. 'Yes, I believe you're right, Rosie. I never looked at it that way.'

'When I said I'd get you to the top I really meant it, Esau, but at first I took the wrong turning by relying too much on your gift. This is another way of doing it: the way that you believe in, too.'

'Good enough.' He patted her arm. 'Business manager from here on, eh? Very well, I'll dash up to London immediately and find out what the trouble is. Whilst I'm gone I should go along and have a look at that cottage if I were you. Take Hilda with you.'

'I'll do just that,' Rose promised.

'Lastly, can I borrow the train fare? I haven't a cent — and that cheque on the table there will hardly do!'

Rose smiled faintly, gave him the

required money, and then with Hilda waving frantically beside her watched Esau Jones depart down the front driveway, his haversack still on his shoulder and panama on the back of his head. At the last moment as he reached the gate he remembered the haversack and got rid of it on to one of the nearby tables — but the old panama was still in position when he later presented himself at the Bureau of Advanced Science and found the usual commissionaire pacing the opulent hall.

'Dr. Haslam?' he repeated, in response to Esau Jones's inquiry. 'Just a moment, sir.'

Mark Haslam had not been back very long — and he certainly wasted no time in joining Esau Jones in the hallway. The look of relief on his face was extraordinary to behold.

'Thank heaven, Mr. Jones — thank heaven!' He pumped Esau's right hand up and down urgently. 'That's all I can think of to say. You've decided to help, of course?'

'For a consideration, yes. I'll tell you

the amount when I've seen what the problem is.'

'Then come this way quickly. It's a terrifying problem, at least to us.'

'Including Dr. Carfax?' Esau Jones asked dryly, as he kept in step beside the physicist.

'Including him, yes. I haven't questioned him yet about the matter you mentioned, but I shall. For the moment this other business is of all-absorbing importance.'

'As far as I am concerned the attempt on my life is of far greater importance, and I'll question Dr. Carfax for myself — later. I allowed his gunmen to go free because they were only tools, but with the guiding brain it will be different.'

Mark Haslam dropped the subject, so did Esau Jones for the time being. But he had no doubts about the fleeting look of consternation that crossed Carfax's austere face when he saw him enter beside Haslam.

'Mr. Jones has had a change of heart, gentlemen!' Mark Haslam exclaimed in delight. 'I am sure all our troubles are over from now on. Oh, do forgive me, Miss Barton, for not including you. Mr. Jones — Miss Barton.'

Esau Jones, panama in hand, inclined his head. 'Stripped down to pure electrons, I notice,' he commented, and the scientists glanced at one another at his lightning appraisal of the secretary's semi-transparent appearance.

'What did I tell you!' Haslam exclaimed. 'He already has the problem at his finger-tips.'

'Not entirely,' Esau Jones corrected. 'Remember that I know your formula to the last detail, Dr. Haslam, and therefore I am pretty well able to assess what has happened — at least to Miss Barton. Later, maybe, you will explain how she comes to be involved in the business?'

'Surely,' Haslam agreed. 'For the moment take a look at the adjoining laboratory — or what remains of it — and see for yourself what we're up against.'

He led the way from the big anteroom and presently Esau Jones found himself studying a remarkably orderly scene of destruction — orderly in that the advancing hole of darkness had sheared everything off clean, leaving a sharp edge between that which had gone and that which remained. The aspect, therefore, was of an immensely wide black hole, which had demolished the walls of the yard to the rear, and the partially wrecked laboratory in the foreground.

'There it is,' Haslam said, his voice grim. 'Chain reaction of the 'nth degree. We've tried every conceivable means of stopping its advance, without success.'

'Pity you didn't heed my warning,' Esau Jones commented dryly.

'That's hardly the point, is it?' Carfax snapped. 'The damage is done and needs rectifying.'

'Name your own figure,' Haslam added.

For a long time Esau Jones was silent, apparently looking at the slowly expanding area. A puzzled expression crossed his face.

'Very peculiar,' he commented at length, looking at the scientists. 'I've tried every formula I know from D to A without producing a result. This is going to demand exclusive work if I'm going to straighten it out.'

Carfax smiled cynically. 'No more than I expected. This is something very different from those glorified conjuring tricks you performed for demonstration, Mr. Jones.'

Esau Jones looked at him sharply. 'That's a lie, Dr. Carfax, and well you know *it*. There was no conjuring attached to my demonstration — '

'Can't we get down to the point?' Haslam broke urgently. 'About this Hole: can you stop it spreading?'

'I can only try. I cannot guarantee success.'

'You can't?' Haslam looked astonished. 'But I understood you to say that you know everything? That all forms of matter obey you?'

'Quite correct, but it should be obvious to you that this is *not* a form of matter. It is the absence of it, hence the necessity for my having to work out a special formula which I'll call A-plus. My charge will be five hundred thousand pounds. Half now and another two hundred-and-fifty thousand when the job is done. If I fail, the initial sum will be returned to you.'

Haslam looked uneasily at Carfax. 'Dr. Carfax is the treasurer of the Bureau,' he explained. 'It's up to him to say what he'll do.'

'Which is easy,' Carfax retorted. 'Nothing! What kind of fools do you take us for, Jones? What's to stop you walking away with the two hundred-and-fifty thousand and never appearing again?'

'The fact that I happen to be an honest man, which is more than you are. Or would you like me to elaborate that statement?'

Carfax hesitated, his face grim, Esau Jones was regarding him blandly.

'I am not in the least interested whether I solve this problem or not,' he said frankly. 'Knowing what I do of matter-control I can, in the last resort, create for myself a space-machine and transport myself and my wife and stepdaughter to another world, there to begin again. So — '

'Just a minute,' Haslam said, alarmed. 'You don't suppose it's going to get so serious that it'll devour the entire world, do you?'

'If unchecked, that is exactly what it will do. I imagine I am the only person likely to prevent that occurrence, but since Dr. Carfax prefers to kill me instead of pay me I'd better withdraw.'

'Kill you!' Carfax echoed. 'What the devil do you mean!'

'If I explain fully it won't be very pleasant for you, Dr. Carfax, will it?' Esau Jones shrugged. 'And I am afraid my sense of justice is such that, unless I receive the fee I have asked for, I shall feel compelled to advise the press how matters stand — concerning the Hole, the fee, and you, Dr. Carfax.'

All the scientists except Haslam looked puzzled. Carfax, knowing that exposure of his effort at murder was being threatened, made an effort to look more amenable.

'Naturally,' he said, 'we have got to have this Hole stopped. You shall have your fee, Mr. Jones, half of it before you go. Now, will you get busy?'

'I can't get busy here. I have to think it out carefully, away from all disturbances.

One thing I will tell you: nothing that has apparently been consumed by this Hole has really been destroyed.'

'Meaning conservation of energy?' Haslam asked.

'Not at all. It is simply that this chain-reaction has produced an undoing of atomic set-ups, therefore destroying the natural appearance, even to the radiation of light-waves. The instant the balance returns everything will snap back to where it was. This is an illusion of matter, if I may call it such.'

'Whatever it is, cure it,' Carfax snapped. 'And whilst we're about it, can you account for Miss Barton being so queerly 'converted' whilst none of us men was affected?'

Esau Jones turned to look at the secretary, and then he smiled.

'For scientists.' he commented, 'you are not very bright. Haven't you learned yet that, for scientific reasons, a woman is regarded as an electron-negative; a man as proton-positive: and an unborn child as neutron, or neutral. This tremendous basic shift in material forces that you brought into being, Dr. Haslam, naturally affected everything predominantly electronic. Hence Miss Barton was transposed into her natural pure electronic state by the outflowing waves; but you men, being protonic, escaped. This change here is definitely associated with electrons because they remain, though stripped, where nothing else does.'

'Yes, that's true enough,' Haslam agreed. 'It conforms with my own deductions, too. That is why I believe only pure protons can restore this Hole to normal — unless, of course, you can produce absolute control. Pure protons are impossible to create, as you know.'

'Difficult,' Esau Jones admitted; 'but I wouldn't say impossible. However, all that has to be worked out. If you will let me have my cheque, gentlemen, I will be on my way. You have my assurance that I'll return the moment I have worked out the formula.'

So, ten minutes later, Esau Jones was on his way back to the station, an extremely thoughtful man. When he reached Little Mereham he had just time to open an account before the bank shut; then he continued on his way to the 'backwoods hotel' to discover Rose in the midst of supervising the sale of unwanted furniture.

'There's a meal in the kitchen,' she told Esau, as he approached. 'Only spot where there's room. I saw the cottage and bought it, which leaves me with about thirty thousand. You were right. It'll do beautifully. How did you get on in London? You were firm about your fee, of course?'

'Yes indeed. Two hundred-and-fifty thousand in the bank, and another two hundred-and-fifty thousand to follow! But there's one snag: if I fail I don't receive a cent and hand all I have straight back.'

'If you fail?' Rose looked at him in wonder. 'But — but that isn't possible, is it? You *couldn't!*'

'For those kind words, many thanks,' he murmured. 'Now I'll go and get that meal.'

He had just finished the meal and was seated thinking, when Rose returned, her furniture supervision at an end. Hilda came dancing in behind her and immediately headed for her Uncle Esau.

'I've been selling the furniture we shan't need,' Rose explained. 'The rest will be moved to the cottage tomorrow and we'll go with it.'

'Which means you've finally decided to resign yourself to life in the country?'

'No, not resign myself. I've come to the conclusion it's the cheapest way of living, and if I need to go to the city I can always do so now and again. Anyhow, it is what you wanted, isn't it?'

'I believe,' Esau Jones said, getting up and putting an arm about her shoulders, 'that we are at last beginning to understand each other, Rosie.'

'Probably.' She gave a rather elusive smile. 'But, Esau, what about this problem you've been asked to solve? Surely there is nothing to stop you?'

'Only one thing: the fact that I'm trying to tackle the absence of matter instead of the presence of it. However, I'll think of something. I shan't let half a million pounds slide by without a mighty fight, believe me. Just leave me alone whilst I worry it out.'

He collected paper from the bureau, then armed with a pencil went out into the leafy front garden and settled himself to work, battered panama on the back of his head. Rose, having enough of her own to deal with, left him to himself, giving strict instructions to Hilda not to disturb her uncle.

But, back in London, things were happening. An occurrence as awe-inspiring as the Hole could not forever be kept quiet, particularly when the second main wall of the yard gave way and a spreading pool of utter black appeared in the main highway as the Hole continued its relentless expansion. By mid-afternoon the early evening papers were full of questions regarding the Hole — questions without answers, for the scientists, relying on Esau Jones to pull something out of the hat, refused to admit how dangerous the Hole really was.

But the secretiveness of the scientists was not good enough for the telephone, gas and electric authorities. With their cables and pipes cut — yet amazingly

160

enough with no gas leaking out of the Hole — they sent gangs of workmen to the site with orders to rush through repair work. The scientists were unaware of this decision until three workmen had endeavoured to get into the Hole, and had completely disappeared along with their equipment. At that the others hung back, bewildered and superstitiously afraid.

Telephones began to ring stridently in the threatened Bureau of Advanced Science as Mark Haslam, on the chance that Esau Jones might fail in his efforts worked desperately to devise a means of scientifically producing pure protons. Carfax, whatever his personal inclinations, was first and foremost a scientist and so helped him. The remaining scientists, their knowledge insufficient to contend with the riddle, had long since departed.

'Damn that 'phone!' Carfax snapped at last — and he went across to it and yanked the instrument from its cradle.

'Yes? Dr. Carfax here — Bureau of Advanced Science.'

'Scotland Yard here, Dr. Carfax — Assistant Commissioner Dale speaking. What's all this business going on in Kensington outside your Bureau? There's a tremendous traffic hold-up, an enormous concentration of people, and some sort of a hole spreading out from the Bureau's main rear yard. If it's an experiment call it off, please. You're causing obstruction.'

'Oh, stop bothering me,' Carfax answered impatiently. 'It's an accident of Nature. Divert all traffic and keep all people away. That Hole is a danger to life — '

'I'm aware of it — and that's why I'm ringing you. Three men from the telephone company have already lost their lives and it's time to explain things.'

'We can't. I've given you all available details: up to you to act on them.'

Annoyed, Carfax rang off, Haslam did not question him because he was deep in calculations, but he had gathered in a subconscious kind of way what all the fuss was about.

However, one cannot have a widening hole of blank nothing travelling across

Kensington without causing violent per-turbation in high quarters. Scotland Yard, considering it had been far too lightly brushed off by the irate Carfax, acted quickly and police patrols were sent to the stricken area. People were clearing away, traffic diverted as Carfax had suggested, and an attempt was made at roping off the Hole. But, inevitably, as it spread, the roping-off became wider and wider and now the swank shops facing the Bureau were threatened with annihilation as the Hole ate its way inexorably towards them.

Assistant Commissioner Dale, informed of all this by radiotelephone, and also anxious to retain his job, sought higher authority. He asked the Chief Commis-sioner, who in turn asked the Home Secretary what he ought to do about it; and since the Home Secretary had not the least idea the Prime Minister was approached.

Finally, in the early evening, as their laboratory was falling to bits around them — the second laboratory in the Bureau to be destroyed by the Hole — Carfax and Haslam were ordered by the last usable 'phone to an audience with the Prime Minister. A car was waiting for them at the rear of the Bureau and it quickly whirled them to Downing Street.

'Since I am mainly responsible for public safety, gentlemen, and because it seems quite impossible to get any sensible statement from anybody else, I am asking you to explain what is happening in Kensington.'

The Prime Minister put it as precisely as that, and since Carfax was obviously determined not to commit himself Haslam had to make the reply.

'It's dangerous, sir, definitely dangerous. That Hole is an area of blank nothing, the opposite of an explosion. In other words, as the Universe was once formed, so it is now being unformed. It's the exact opposite of creation. It's — de-creation, if I may use the word.'

'Use what word you like, Dr. Haslam. It's got to stop. Do you realize how much trouble it's causing?'

'Yes. But it can't be stopped. I'd have sent out warnings earlier if I hadn't been so preoccupied in trying to get the trouble in hand. You see, it's something that never happened before. However, I remain sanguine that within a couple of days the problem will be overcome.'

'You seem to be contradicting yourself, Dr. Haslam,' the Prime Minister reminded him. 'You just said it couldn't be stopped, and now you refer to overcoming the problem.'

'I meant that I have an expert dealing with it. In two days he'll be ready to act — maybe sooner.'

'From the Bureau of Advanced Science, you mean?'

'No. He's a — a lone worker. Very good grasp of material laws.'

'His name?'

'Esau Jones.'

'Never heard of him,' the Prime Minister said brusquely. 'What are his qualifications? He *is* a qualified scientist, of course?'

'No — a dabbler,' Carfax put in sourly. 'But he seems to know his stuff.'

'Listen to me, gentlemen,' the Prime Minister said seriously. 'This position is extremely dangerous: you have admitted that. Property and human lives are in jeopardy and, admitting that you your-selves cannot grapple with the difficulty, you mention an outsider whom nobody has ever heard of and who hasn't any academic qualifications. I forbid you to employ such a person. He'll only make matters worse.'

'Far from it!' Haslam cried in alarm. 'Indeed, he is our only chance, sir, believe me!'

'From your point of view, perhaps so, but I have the public to consider — and it certainly will not accept an unknown trying to put this business right. My decision stands. Make a report to the Central Scientific Association immedi-ately, explaining what has occurred, and the best brains of every country can go to work right away.'

'It won't make a jot of difference!' Haslam protested. 'I know exactly what caused this trouble because I started it, and if even I can't find the answer, how can other scientists?'

'Yet you think a dabbler can? This — whatever his name is?'

'You must have read, or heard, of his demonstration in the Bureau of Advanced Science a couple of nights ago?' Haslam insisted.

'Come to think of it I do recall something of that nature,' the Prime Minister admitted. 'But a glorified magical act has little relation to the disintegration created by that Hole!'

'It was not a glorified magical act: that was simply the brainless way in which unscientific reporters explained things. Esau Jones is the absolute master of matter, and he's the only man in the world who can solve this problem.'

The Prime Minister shook his head. 'That isn't good enough for me, Dr. Haslam. Do as I have instructed and tell this Jones person that he need exert himself no further. Meanwhile I will have the B.B.C. and the other stations broadcast a warning, together with reassurances that the Central Scientific Association is at work. That is my decision, gentlemen.'

To go against it was impossible since the Prime Minister had the final word, so with as much grace as they could muster Haslam and Carfax departed, looking at one another when they were once again in Downing Street.

'Only thing we can do now is go and hurry Jones up,' Haslam said resolutely. 'Be hanged to what the Prime Minister says. He's talking of something right outside his province.'

'You can't do it, Haslam — and you know it. If you dare to use Jones now he'll be picked up by the authorities and jailed. They won't let him get anywhere near that Hole — not that I believe he can do anything even if he does.'

'If you believe that, why did you pay him two hundred-and-fifty thousand pounds? Was it to keep him quiet, so he wouldn't expose the fact you tried to murder him with a couple of your trained gorillas?'

'Bluntly — yes. I still don't think he possesses the powers he pretends to have.'

'Then why did you go to the effort, and risk, of trying to have him wiped out? You told me, when you tried to drag me into your schemes, that you believed he had enough power to dissolve the world, if need be.'

'And at that time I meant it. Since then I have seen how impotent he is — when faced with that Hole, for instance. If he is the master of matter that he claims to be he'd have put it right there and then and cleaned up his full half million. As it is he's got half the amount and has disappeared in order to think it out. I don't believe we'll ever see him again.'

'We've got to! We can't allow the Bureau to lose two hundred-and-fifty thousand for nothing!'

'I'll reimburse the Bureau,' Carfax said. 'I consider that as hush money to keep Jones quiet. My reputation must be kept clear.'

By this time they had come to the corner of Downing Street. Carfax was calling for a taxi to take them to the Bureau, but Haslam shook his head.

'Not much point in that, Carfax. The situation is out of our hands now, and the Bureau is pretty well wrecked anyway or will be within a few hours. The police, under the order of the Prime Minister, will be in control from now on. No, I'm going to find Jones and ginger him up. It's on my way home anyway. My car's at the Whitehall Garage. I left it there for a minor repair this morning. Good job I did or it might have gone into the Hole whilst we were computing in the laboratory.'

'Up to you,' Carfax said briefly. 'But let him keep that cheque. I'll repay it into the funds.'

'If Jones is as honest as I believe him to be he'll make me take it back. Believe me, Carfax, I'll do nothing to protect you. You deserve exposure.'

Carfax gave him a bitter glance and then turned away. Haslam went in the opposite direction to the Whitehall Garage.

7

Miss Barton to the rescue

It was nearly half-past ten on that calm summer night when Mark Haslam's powerful Jaguar drew up outside the 'backwoods' hotel. Esau Jones, lounging at one of the tables in the front garden, seemed half asleep. Upon the table was a half-consumed glass of beer and a pile of papers. He stirred quickly enough, however, at the sound of Haslam's footsteps.

'Why, Dr. Haslam!' Esau Jones got to his feet. 'What's this? Things got worse?'

'Infinitely!' Haslam sat at the table contemplatively smoothing his homburg with his jacket cuff. 'That blasted Hole is right across Kensington. I've called in on my way home to find out how far you've got.'

Esau Jones spread his hands. 'Nowhere. Care for a glass of beer? The wife'll fix it.

She's inside preparing for a removal — '

'Never mind the beer, man, thanks all the same. What do you mean by 'nowhere'?'

'Just what I say. See these papers? I've been working on the problem ever since I got back here, but I just can't devise a formula. It's that business of reasoning from nothing into something. I've never done it before. Always reasoned from the opposite standpoint. Like trying to write left-handed when you're right-handed,' Esau Jones finished gloomily.

'Then — what happens?' Haslam asked, plainly horrified.

'I give you your money back, earn my wife's profound displeasure, and admit there is a scientific problem I can't solve. Pity, but there it is.'

'The answer is in protons,' Haslam insisted. 'If only we could get enough of them to put into that area I know we'd restore everything right back instantly. The chain-reaction would be stopped because there'd be instant electrical balance. Can't you think how to create protons?'

172

Esau Jones reflected. 'I — might. I doubt it, though. In the case of protons, as with electrons, it demands a knowledge of what they exactly comprise. Nobody knows for sure. They're merely rated as electrical charges of inconceivable minuteness, and that's mighty flimsy material to work on. So much different from matter entire; I have a mental picture beforehand and the force of thought I bring to bear makes it materialize. Atoms and aggregates just drop into place, products of objectified mental waves. But whoever saw a proton or an electron to know what they look like and create them individually? It comes down to this, Dr. Haslam: I can only create matter as far as I can visualize it. If it can't be visualized I can't form the mental pattern. Obvious, isn't it? Hence the difficulty of creating a proton — or mass of protons. Hence also the difficulty of restoring that negative state existing in the Hole. Though I can produce anything of which I can think, thus — '

Esau Jones stopped for a moment and pointed through a clear gap in the tall hedge towards the distant meadow. Haslam looked and gave a start as a replica of the Taj Mahal appeared in a flash in the dying evening light, to vanish almost as quickly.

'I am lost when I delve in to the ultimates of matter,' Esau Jones finished, despondent.

'Then here's a suggestion. Throw overboard your creative gift for the moment and instead let's concentrate on how to create protonic streams by normal scientific methods. You say you know all there is to know about science, so let's get busy. I'm willing. I'll work all night if need be, but a result we've got to have.'

'No harm in trying,' Esau Jones agreed, rising to his feet. 'We'd better go inside and tell the wife we're going to burn midnight oil. I'll see your car goes into the converted stable at the back there and prevent road obstruction.'

Haslam nodded and got to his feet, then he watched with helpless fascination as his Jaguar deliberately started up its engine and, guided by an invisible hand, came up the drive, turned the corner, and vanished in the converted stable nearby.

'I like that sort of mental exercise now and again,' Esau Jones explained, collecting his notes. 'Just assures me I am not losing my grip.'

'You're certainly not doing that!' Haslam said. 'Have you a 'phone here? I must ring my wife.'

'In the hall. Help yourself.'

This matter had been attended to by the time Rose had been told what was afoot. Still evidently resolved to cling to her change of heart she raised no objections, leaving the two men to themselves in the lounge and retiring to bed early in readiness for a hard day's work on the morrow.

'Scanty furniture, but enough,' Esau Jones grinned. 'If it isn't I'll produce some more. And we need electric light.'

It appeared, bright and clear, in the center of the ceiling and the two men sat down and began discussion. Now and again a glass of beer appeared magically at Esau Jones's elbow, and was presently supplemented by coffee and sandwiches, which Haslam consumed. So they argued and figured, and argued again, trying a theory, discarding it, trying another.

'Incidentally,' Haslam said, after an interval of quiet, 'the Government has ordered me to stop you working on this problem, but I've such faith in you I've ignored the edict. May make it difficult for you, though, if they try to stop you by force.'

Esau Jones grinned. 'If I get the right idea it will take more than the Government to stop me.'

'*If* you do. We're a long way off yet, apparently.'

'Now, I wonder — ' Esau Jones sank his chin on his chest and pushed out his feet. 'The answer may be simpler than we think. Tell me — has that secretary girl got a boy friend?'

'What?' Haslam stared blankly. 'You mean Miss Barton?'

'That's the girl! The one who's gone transparent. Has she a fiancé?'

'I never asked her.' Haslam winced slightly. 'Knowing her tremendous scientific interests, I doubt it. She's no clinging vine.'

'She's a woman,' Esau Jones said, raising a finger. 'For that perfectly logical reason it is possible some man somewhere has seen in her his ideal, from a scientific angle or otherwise. Can you get her on the 'phone?'

'I imagine so, yes — at her home. But — What the devil are you driving at? We're searching for protons!'

'I know. That's the point. Try and get Miss Barton.'

Bewildered, Haslam obeyed the order and went into the hall. He was absent some five minutes. When he returned he gave a nod.

'Yes, she's got a boy friend — in fact a fiancé. She says she wears an engagement ring, but I've never noticed it. I think she thought I was crazy asking such a question. She said that I, as a married man, ought to have known better.'

Esau Jones gave a yell of laughter.

'It isn't funny,' Haslam observed sourly. 'In fact it's a completely irrelevant inquiry in the midst of our troubles.'

'On the contrary, ring Miss Barton again, tell her to get her fiancé, and have the pair of them come over here right away.'

'But dammit, man, it's early morning!'

'I don't care if it's the crack of doom — get 'em!'

Completely lost, but still willing to obey the genius in corduroy trousers, Haslam did as he was told. When he returned he gave a violent start as he beheld complicated electronic equipment standing close beside the table.

'Where on earth did this lot come from?' he demanded.

'Formula D,' Esau Jones replied absently. 'Are they coming?'

'Yes — but Miss Barton doesn't like the idea.'

'That is immaterial. You observe here, Dr. Haslam, electronic equipment of the most advanced kind, in fact so advanced that it doesn't exist anywhere in the world except here. All we need now is a chunk of *infiniform*. Let me see, you *did* say every element in the Periodic Table, didn't you? Yes, I remember the formula clearly.'

There was a sudden clink and a chunk

of *infiniform* appeared on a small ledge beneath one of the instruments. Haslam gave an uneasy look.

'Now wait a minute, Jones, what are you getting at? Glancing around me I'd say you aim to disintegrate a chunk of *infiniform* just as I did, except that your instruments are designed differently from mine.'

'Correct,' Esau Jones agreed amiably.

'But you can't do it! That's the very thing I did, and look what happened!'

'You did not take proper precautions, Dr. Haslam — but I shall! All we have to do now is await the arrival of Miss Barton and her illustrious boy friend.'

Haslam opened his mouth and shut it again. There were a host of questions he wanted to ask, but he could see from Esau Jones's expression that he would not answer them. Indeed he had just created another glass of beer and was draining it in deep satisfaction.

'Don't look so distressed, man,' he reproved, setting down the glass. 'The problem is solved, you know — completely, and I shall be able to make Dr.

Carfax pay up to the uttermost penny.'

'Solved? I see precious little sign of it.'

'You will. It is not so entirely solved by one of my mental formulae as by a scientific law. Who cares, just so long as we have the answer?'

Haslam sat down and the next half hour sat screwing up his forehead and gazing in space as he struggled to comprehend what the wonder man was talking about.

Then the echoes were awakened as Miss Barton and her boy friend hammered on the front door of the practically empty place. Immediately Esau Jones went and admitted them, directing them into the lounge. Miss Barton was still dressed in the same clothes in which she had met with her accident — and she was also still semi-transparent and very irritated.

'Dr. Haslam, what is the meaning of this?' she demanded. 'At this hour of the night, too!'

'I am the culprit, Miss Barton,' Esau Jones apologized, and then glanced inquiringly at the tall, broad-shouldered young man who looked like a professional footballer.

'Larry Deakin,' Miss Barton said briefly. 'Mr. Jones, and Dr. Haslam.'

Larry Deakin had a bone-cracking handshake and a puzzled look.

'Gents, I'm no scientist,' he said frankly. 'I leave all that bunk — I mean knowledge, to Amy here. We've a mutual agreement to forget all about science when we're together. But right at this moment we're neck-deep in the stuff. I've been plaguing Amy to tell me why she looks like a ghost, but she won't say.'

'Very shortly, young man, you will also look like a ghost,' Esau Jones said calmly.

'Huh?' Larry's eyes popped.

'But it will not be for long. Tell me, Mr. Deakin, are you really in love with — er — this young lady?'

'More'n anything in the world, yes.'

'How interesting! In that case you will be more than willing to restore your fiancée to normal? To rid her of her ghostly appearance?'

'Definitely! But how does that link up with me looking like her?'

'You will see shortly. I propose, Miss Barton,' Esau Jones continued, addressing himself to the girl, 'to use you and Mr. Deakin to undo the unfortunate experiment attempted by Dr. Haslam. You will be quite unhurt, and probably will gain everlasting fame for having saved the world from slow and relentless dissolution.'

Miss Barton shrugged. 'I'm willing to do what I can, but I cannot follow your reasoning.'

'Few can,' Esau Jones chuckled. 'Sometimes I even wonder myself what the blazes I'm talking about. However — if you will be so kind as to step over here, Mr. Deakin?'

Larry Deakin did as he was told, nonetheless looking vaguely nervous, and finished up within three feet of the motionless chunk of *infiniform*.

'Now,' Esau Jones said, hands in trouser pockets. 'Let me outline. You, Dr. Haslam, produced a pure electron state by the disintegration of your original *infiniform*. Right?'

'Unfortunately — very right!'

'We are seeking pure protons,' Esau Jones continued. 'In the scientific law a male body represents that order of make-up. What stumped me was where to get enough protons for our purpose to balance the electrons, for we have quite a considerable Hole of Nothing to restore to normal. Then it occurred to me that if we can only get a focusing point of balance, wherein protons and electrons, both in the pure state, arrive *together* in the Hole, the preponderance will instantly restore normalcy, on the same principle that a tiny pebble thrown into a big lake can disturb the entire surface.'

'Where,' Haslam asked, with unnatural calm, 'do we get the protons?'

'Mr. Deakin is the answer to that. I'm going to turn him into pure protons, just as Miss Barton is already pure electrons.'

'But you can't!' Haslam objected. 'My *infiniform*, when exploded, produces an *electronic* chain-reaction, not protonic.'

'In your formula for *infiniform* you overlooked the transuranic elements,' Esau Jones said. 'They are unstable, as you know, and normally can only be created for fractions of a second. I, however, having a complete mastery of all things material, have added them into the *infiniform* and the mathematics thereof show definitely that protons will be produced on this occasion, and not electrons. There's nothing uncanny about that. The presence or absence of an ingredient in any particular substance does of course change its nature and effects. Now, let us see what we can do. Just stay exactly where you are, Mr. Deakin, and remember — science will applaud you.'

'Or bury me,' Larry responded uneasily.

Esau Jones took good care to place himself, Miss Barton and Dr. Haslam behind a tall neutralizing screen before he switched on the current. Instantly there was a blinding flash from the *infiniform*, and it promptly vanished. Larry Deakin staggered a few paces and then pulled up short. Instantly Esau Jones closed another switch and there followed a tremendous electrical surge through the lounge. Then all was quiet again.

'That,' Esau Jones remarked, 'is that. We might as well be rid of this stuff.'

He looked at the apparatus and every trace of it vanished. Larry Deakin blinked, then looked at his hands. He could see straight through them. Every part of him was as glass-like as Miss Barton herself.

'Neither you, Mr. Deakin, or you, Miss Barton, are to touch each other,' Esau Jones warned. 'Otherwise you'll spoil all our good work. And you and I, Dr. Haslam, will not touch either of them. They are 'primed', so to speak, for the final move.'

'I assume Larry is protons and Miss Barton electrons?' Haslam asked, very tired but with eyes still wide open in wonder.

'Correct.'

'Then tell me one thing: why didn't that *infiniform* chunk you just blew up start a chain-reaction in protons, instead of electrons?'

'Because the special electrical surge I switched on a fraction afterwards counteracted that possibility.'

185

'If I may ask something,' Miss Barton interposed. 'Why go to all this trouble to create of Larry a purely protonic man when this apparatus of yours — which you possessed a moment ago — could just as easily have taken care of the Hole?'

'It couldn't.' Esau Jones answered. 'It did not project protons: it merely annihilated a substance which radiated the correct frequency to reduce an object — in this case, Mr. Deakin — to protons. The final act comes in the morning at daybreak.'

He peered into space and four beds, perfectly made, came abruptly into view in the four corners of the room. He grinned and motioned to them, then added:

'And remember! You two must not touch each other, nor must we touch you.'

★ ★ ★

Rose, when she prepared breakfast the following morning, was more amenable than ever when she learned that her

186

husband had solved the mystery of the Hole and without sacrificing his principles. Nonetheless she did not concern herself with accompanying the four to London in Mark Haslam's car: she had the final details of removal to attend to.

The London journey was awkward. Larry Deakin sat in the spacious boot and Miss Barton at the rear of the car, Esau Jones sitting next to Haslam. Thereby separateness was observed. On the way Esau Jones gave final instructions.

'Since I'm out of this by Government order, Dr. Haslam, you must take over. Find out exactly the position of that Hole in Kensington, and also determine where a manhole shaft exists to reach the sewage system.'

'What?' Haslam asked blankly.

'You must do as I say,' the wonder man insisted, 'otherwise our two young friends will cancel out this Hole and then find themselves crushed to death by solids returning abruptly to normal. It's essential that they be in a space that is normally open — like a manhole shaft. Its position must be *absolutely* determined, and a helicopter will do the rest.'

Haslam saw the point, and once London was reached he went into action, stopping the car about a quarter of a mile from the police cordon that marked the outer perimeter of the still silently expanding Hole.

Esau Jones remained in the car, as did Miss Barton and Larry Deakin. As far as Esau Jones was concerned, there was no action the police could take. If he did not actively participate, they were powerless.

Haslam wasted no time in making things move. He found all the information Esau Jones had instructed him to get, and was then given the helicopter he required. All the available scientists were also summoned by him, including Dr. Carfax, to watch the banishment of the Hole from existence, which seemed now a tall order considering its extent. So, an imposing array of officials, from Scotland Yard, the Government, and science's highest realms — together with thousands of gaping sightseers and the media

— watched the most remarkable happening London had ever witnessed.

The helicopter, containing the pilot and — on the end of a cable and cradle — Larry Deakin and Miss Barton, flew to the point exactly charted as the position of a manhole-shaft, and here the protonic man and electronic woman, still separate, were lowered gently in the suspended cradle down towards the Hole, the helicopter remaining motionless. Abruptly the bottom of the cradle disappeared and Larry and Miss Barton dropped into the Hole. At this point Esau Jones came into action. Standing on the roof of the Jaguar, using a mat so that his clumsy boots would not scratch the black cellulose, he suddenly bawled:

'Hug each other, you two!'

Police looked suspiciously at him, officials demurred, and then something like a thunderclap deafened everybody for a second. At the instant Larry and Miss Barton embraced the Hole vanished. Everything was back as though it had never been disturbed, which in actual fact it had not. Light-waves returned to normal and solidities were in their accustomed places. And, down in the depths of a manhole-shaft, were Larry and Miss Barton, out of sight because of the sudden reappearance of the manhole cover, but there was no hesitation in yanking the cover out of the way.

Embarrassed and dirty, but entirely solid, the young man and woman emerged from the hole into the midst of the surging crowd.

'So,' Esau Jones commented, as at length Haslam reached him, 'the balance was struck when proton and electron united in the purely electronic area. Which reminds me, Dr. Carfax,' he added, turning to the saturnine physicist, 'that you owe me a cheque. I'll take it now.'

Carfax tightened his lips, but he had no alternative but to comply. Esau Jones smiled as he put the cheque in his pocket.

'I thank you — and you need have no fear, Dr. Carfax. Your imprudence towards me will never be mentioned. Now I must be going — '

'But you can't!' Haslam exclaimed.

'The Government knows you restored things because I told them so. You'll be honoured — '

'No thanks. I'm a countryman, and besides I have an appointment in the magistrates' court at Godalming.'

On that Esau Jones quickly turned away and vanished in the crowd. When he arrived at the cottage in mid-afternoon he found Rose and Hilda amidst the dumped furniture and a pot of tea had just been prepared.

'Well?' Rose asked, as Esau Jones came in. 'How did things go?'

'Splendidly. In London that Hole was put right, and in court I was only fined a relatively small sum for a technical transgression of the law, but it does leave me free to create as many cars and trailers on the original design as I wish. So I think that's what I'll do legally. I got my remaining two hundred-and-fifty thousand from Carfax this morning. So there it is, my dear. I'll go into the car and trailer business. As to my gift: well, I only need to use it when folks get in such a jam they can't get out.'

Rose smiled seriously. 'Just as you wish, Esau, now you have plenty of money. But didn't London thank you for what you did?'

'I dunno. Maybe we'll find out later.'

They did. For weeks, radio, newspapers and television spoke of the wonder man and lauded him to the skies. But he was not interested. Nothing could tempt him back to the city. All he wanted was his beer, the country air, Rose and little Hilda, and the chance to create cars and trailers how and when he chose.

THE END